SHIVERING, Erica stood listening. The silence was a little frightening. She could not guess how late it was. All the doors along the hall were closed. It was like being left alone in an empty house—no, not an *empty* house—rather one inhabited by someone—or something—she would rather not meet. Her hand was on the knob of her door, ready to close it.

And then she heard the footsteps on the stairs . . . footsteps with an oddly long pause between each. *And against her will she was drawn down the shadowed corridor. . . .*

SNOW SHADOW

Andre
Norton

FAWCETT CREST • NEW YORK

SNOW SHADOW

Published by Fawcett Crest Books, a unit of CBS Publications, the Consumer Publishing Division of CBS Inc.

Printed in the United States of America

10 9 8 7 6 5 4 3 2 1

1

Perhaps not many people nowadays know those old sayings which have become so trite they are cast aside. Do bad beginnings lead to good endings? Our modern pessimism would perhaps deny that. I certainly had acquired some knowledge of a few things *not* to do the second time I came to Ladensville. As my taxi bored through the dusk of a wet post-Thanksgiving evening, I made myself resurrect some memories of past snares, delusions, and my own folly, which should have made me cringe.

Such self-torment was, I decided, second-thoughting, one of the things I must leave behind me. It must not be allowed to spoil my present slow-stirring enthusiasm or scratch the shell, which, I flattered myself I had successfully grown.

I did not have to be any longer embarrassed for that

other Erica Jansen, who had been full of futile envy for her bright, assured contemporaries, who had left her far behind in a struggle for social acceptance. Earlier, I had been out of step with the new rebels. Even their language had been a foreign tongue (and I am no linguist)—since I had been shaped to the pattern drawn up by Aunt Otilda, so hedged in by her iron-bar control that I had not even dared to look beyond the code of behavior which had been pounded into my mind from the time I could understand anything at all.

When Aunt Otilda had finally relinquished the reins of our lives (through a heart attack, which must have angered her even as she died), I had tried to break down my walls, sensing that I must do so or never learn to live at all. My life was not a collection of *dos*—rather a prison of *don't*s. Only I had had no idea how one *could* escape. So even now, my efforts to join the world still consisted of rather timid venturings out, and quick retreats.

A recent modest success in my writing had given me a small measure of confidence, which I had thought gone, after the cruel hurt I had known in this same Ladensville. But I sensed that I either fought back *now*, or I would go under completely and never have a life of my own.

Memory was like biting on an aching tooth. But now, as I tentatively tried evoking it, there was no stab to follow. Only a lingering trace of resentment and shame—shame at having been just the gullible fool Aunt Otilda had always declared that I was. Thank heaven she had never learned of my folly! I held to the thought that all that had happened to another person.

The Erica Jansen of five years ago was not the girl of today. The earlier one was safely dead, and I would keep her buried.

My freedom was what counted. I could meet who I pleased, go where I wanted. It was that freedom which led me now to this journey through a thick and dreary moisture, which was a stand-in for snow. It was running into Theodosia Cantrell today, and summoning up the nerve to speak to her, our chatter over coffee producing tonight's invitation. With the anticipation of meeting those whose interests might be said to match mine, I looked through the window of the taxi, at slush which took on the glitter of pre-Christmas snow.

This section of the Maryland college town was new to me. The street lights seemed to be set farther apart, the spaces between them unusually dark and shadowed. I suddenly wondered what kind of a crime rate Ladensville might have. Those patches of dark could well attract muggers. Or had that insidious violence not yet seeped out this far from Washington, some miles away?

Though I knew well, after a steady flow of disillusionment, that with me anticipation always outran realization, I did look forward to this evening. Theodosia was a blazing star in a field where my own accomplishment might be likened to the flare of a match. I envied her, in an impersonal way, for a fine talent, the polished craftsmanship, her apparent ability to produce a steady flow of subtle crimes-of-the-past novels, which were always book-club choices, early climbers on the bestseller lists.

I admired her thick plait of dull red hair, her distinc-

tively plain face which outshone the merely pretty, her
warm friendliness and that utter lack of the self-con-
sciousness which poisoned my own attempts at social
contacts. Tonight I was both flattered and a little
thrilled at being asked to join the kind of circle I felt
sure she gathered about her.

My cab pulled into a side street, where walled gardens
concealed most of the houses. Its pace was now a
crawl.

"This the place, lady?"

For a moment I shared my driver's doubt. The
building was a lightless cube, looking, in this sleety
dusk, even sinister. Then I remembered the directions.
"Go up that drive. I want the carriage house—in the
rear."

Dark shrubbery looped to the sodden ground, forming a frosted jungle. The dark house was that of Theodosia's landlady, the Mrs. Emma Horvath who was at
present in a nursing home. The driver and I passed under the arch of a portico and came into a courtyard,
where small lamps, on either side of a door painted
bright red, defied the storm with their light.

That light and the warming color of the door raised
my spirits so that I used the polished brass knocker
with more than my usual energy. Theodosia answered
my summons, and I had a moment of disquiet, as if I
had been too forceful. Was it a trick of the lantern
light, or had there been a shade of irritation on her
face? But the warmth of her greeting dispelled my
vague doubts.

As I shed my rain-repelling scarf before the mirror
in the very small entry, I caught on the mirror's glassy

surface, behind my own dark hair and undistinguished features, a revealing glimpse of my hostess. Shadows, perhaps produced by the wrong perspective, deepened hollows beneath her prominent cheekbones, giving her a haggard, beaten look. But when I restored my lipstick to my bag and swung around, she was as I had always seen her, untroubled and vividly alive.

The room beyond was large and, at first glance, seemed filled with people. A hearthfire drew me, as fires always have. This one provided a frame for three guests who sat directly before it, their backs to the door. To the left, a slight, fair-haired man maneuvered a portable bar between two chairs, the occupants of which appeared to consider him invisible, continuing their conversation over and around him.

That old, constricting feeling—of being odd woman out—arose to daunt me again in spite of my resolutions. Just as I wanted to slip away, Theodosia's fingers were warm on my arm, and she drew me to the trio by the fireplace.

Three heads, gray, blond, and tawny brown, turned slightly. The blonde showed the finished touch of an accomplished hairdresser—coaxed into the carefully casual style which means money in any woman's mind. It was as short as a masculine crop might be, but, as my hostess brought me to face the three, I could see no one would ever mistake the sex of the tall girl between the two men. I mentally set my teeth against being withered by the supreme self-confidence of a woman who used all the power of her sex.

She demanded attention with her arrogance of manner, the power of her clever, exotic face, the poise of her well-tended body. She was lacquered—polished. No. Those descriptive words meant careful rubbing with soft cloths; there was nothing soft or rubbed about Leslie Lowndes. She was faceted! I was proud of the adjective my imagination had supplied.

Burnished as a gemstone, wearing her thick hair in a style few women of her age would be courageous enough to try, her sleek figure given discreet emphasis by a stark black pants suit cut in next season's line, she was at ease. Her features were not faultless—her nose a shade too large, her expertly made-up mouth thin-lipped. But she rendered colorless every other woman near her.

Her present companions were in contrast to each other. The tawny-haired giant to her right cupped a cocktail glass in a hand which could easily have engulfed a decanter. He arose to greet me with a stiff little bow. His face wore a serious, slightly worried expression, and I believed that the lines of his wide mouth and square chin spelled stubbornness without much humor. When Theodosia said "Hanno Horvath," he sketched a second bow.

The third member of the gathering was a small man, or perhaps of average height made to seem less in that company. He was clearly a generation older than his companions, his gray hair close matched in color to his gray suit. Beside Leslie's sleekness and the suggestion of brute strength which emanated from Horvath, he should have been dwarfed and colorless. But he was not. When I met his lively eyes, mirroring interest and welcome, and noted lines of humor at the corners of those eyes and about the lips shadowed by a neatly trimmed, British-style mustache, I was both attracted and reassured.

Privately, I always thought that circulation at such parties would be immeasurably improved if the guests wore badges. Not those name-tags beloved by conventions, but rather ones reading, "I do this or that." Such would provide opening gambits for small talk.

The name the gray gentleman bore—Preston Donner—meant nothing to me. But I had a feeling that he outranked his present company in ways which really mattered—just as his quick, yet not obtrusive, courtesy was in contrast to Miss Lowndes' cool stare and murmur, and Horvath's bow.

"Theo—" Leslie's drawl dismissed me. "You've worked wonders with this place. It always had charm, but poor Irene had no imagination—her idea of the light touch—" She shuddered with a studied movement of her shoulders. "Not that it must have been easy for her to move out, when Miss Emma changed her mind."

I felt rather than saw Theodosia tense. "The changing about of some chairs and one sofa, both belonging to Mrs. Horvath," she observed dryly, "can scarcely be termed an outstanding feat of interior decoration. Also had we—had *I*," she corrected herself swiftly, "known of the circumstance under which this house was vacated, we would not, I assure you, be here now."

She was, I was certain, not only answering what she considered an impertinence on Leslie's part, but somehow making plain to the others her stand in some problem.

Leslie laughed. "Miss Emma wanted you here, and

since she always gets what she wants, that settled it. And she had set Irene out, even before Gordon made such an impression on her sympathy with his story of your house-hunting woes. Of course Irene did not like it. As if her troubles matter."

She was watching Theodosia over the glass Leslie turned around and around. Her malice was nearly open. Even I could read it, as the tip of her tongue swept across her lower lip. She looked then as if she savored some delicious taste, before she added:

"As I said, Miss Emma gets what she wants—and always has. From Alexis Horvath's millions to any tame escort she fancies. You'll learn that when she is in residence again. She gets what she wants or raises hell." Her tone was light, blt there was a hidden note in it, suggesting that was not only a warning, but in some way a threat.

Preston Donner cut through a tense moment of silence. He drew up a chair for me and coughed, a little deprecatingly, before he spoke.

"Miss Irene understands your complete innocence in the matter, Mrs. Cantrell. She was and is distressed over the sudden loss of what she considered her home, as is only natural. It was her impression, and that of the family, that this house was an outright gift on the occasion of her marriage to Miss Emma's nephew. Though the deed did not change hands, it was thought unnecessary in a family transaction. A pity that." He shook his head. "Miss Emma's poor health has led to more than one sudden, unfortunate misunderstanding."

"You mean airing of dislikes." Leslie cut in. She apparently had no intention of any oil being poured on waters which she desired to remain troubled. "One of which being small children. You'd think these were museum pieces." She drew fingertips along the arm of the settee on which she sat. "The way she went on about possible damage after Stuart began to walk! Though Miss Elizabeth feels somewhat the same—to both of them things mean more than people—

"Yes, when Irene produced Stuart, and Charles was no longer a decorative naval officer but became a fixture in the hospital, Miss Emma changed her mind in a hurry. She's been discussing will changes, too, hasn't she? She wants attention, gallants clustering around. Hanno—Charles—" Leslie smiled. "You need not worry about *your* being dispossessed in a hurry, Theo—not with Gordon in evidence. And your stay here *is* only temporary, isn't it?"

"It is indefinite." Theodosia's reply was sharp, but her tone brought about no shadow of change in Leslie's bland expression as she smiled at her hostess. They might be exchanging meaningless chatter appropriate to the occasion.

Preston Donner turned to me with what was clearly a firm intention of changing the subject.

"You are certainly the Erica Jansen who gave us that very readable biography of Mrs. Southworth last year." He stated that as if my small splash into the pond of the publishing world had caused a tidal wave, and now my writer's vanity awoke.

But all I could say was yes, and that I was pleased to know he found my book acceptable.

"In my opinion you handled the problem of the

lady's missing husband very skillfully. At a time when it was a disgrace to be a deserted wife, no matter how innocent, such details must have been suppressed nearly beyond the power of a modern researcher to uncover. You must meet Miss Elizabeth Austin. Her mother was a friend of Mrs. Southworth's—in her latter days, naturally. People were doubtful of the lady's respectability even then. What a queerly unbalanced sense of morality they did subscribe to. More often the innocent were punished instead of the guilty."

"So the Austins called, in spite of an ambiguous missing husband?" Leslie commented. "How tolerant of them."

"Who is Miss Elizabeth Austin?" I asked. Again I wanted labels, not names. And I was uneasy at the tension I felt.

Donner had leaned forward as if to launch into explanation when Theodosia stepped away and caught the sleeve of the fair-haired man who had earlier been struggling with the bar.

Beside her, he lost both color and presence. His soft mouth, certainly too curved for a man (A man should have—then I censored my thoughts. No comparisons now or ever again) was set in a near-petulant pout. He could have been a sulky son forced into some social gesture by a dominant mother, whose interference in his life he heartily detested but did not have the will to combat.

I guessed at his age, and then made hasty correction as I caught those lines about the eyes, a little too knowing for my taste. The college boy of my first estimate had certainly been a number of years off-campus.

"Erica, this is Gordon." Theodosia made the introduction swiftly.

Gordon Cantrell—the few facts I knew about him did not quite match the man holding a tray of glasses in my general direction. An illustrator who had had shows in New York, so popular when he married Theodosia that it had been his name, and not hers, which had made the wedding an item for gossip columns. It was hard to match that to this sulking figure.

I produced a company smile, accepted a glass, but he had turned away before my murmured greeting was complete. The firelight pointed up the slight puffiness under his eyes, the blurring of jawline. He brushed past Donner to stand before Leslie. She set her glass back on the tray—but something about his attitude suggested—

My imagination was straying out of bounds tonight. I gave myself a mental shake. First that feeling induced by the unlighted Horvath house looming through the dark of a stormy early evening, now undercurrents I thought I detected here—reading tension even in the way a glass might be set upon a tray!

Theodosia had slipped away. Hanno Horvath, sunk in what appeared to be a state of dark brooding, had slipped well down in his chair, his long legs thrusting forth to the very edge of the hearth. Now Leslie stared into the flames as if she were utterly alone, the rest of us wiped out of her state of existence.

Preston Donner again broke an awkward silence. I was not even aware he had gone and returned until he presented a dish of canapes at my elbow.

"I recommend the small pink ones, Miss Jansen.

They have a most intriguing flavor. And the horns contain shrimp paste—"

I relaxed determinedly. His deference sprang from the secure manners of Aunt Otilda's world, in which I had been bred, and I liked the man.

"Do I detect a prejudice against shrimp paste?" I refused to be cowed into silence—as I once might have been—by Leslie's attitude.

"Allergies are always one's bane. Yes, fish and I must keep apart."

We drifted into book talk, and so I discovered that Donner was a dealer in rare editions, who made periodic trips to Ladensville to confer with the head of the Grachian Trust Library at the university. His period by choice was the early nineteenth century, and soon we were engrossed to the point of interrupting each other with comment or stories of discoveries, until we were summoned to a buffet supper.

Preston Donner dealt quickly and competently with the filling of plates, and then shepherded me back as if he had cut out some prize he was determined to keep to himself. I bloomed a little. He was so manifestly interested in *me*—a situation I had not found to be true very often.

"No American to rival Jane Austen—" I continued our discussion.

"So you are a Janite, too! But how fortunate. Right over there," he so forgot manners as to use his fork for a pointer, "lies Northanger Abbey."

I blinked. The word "abbey" for a connoisseur of Victorian fiction has a meaning all its own, including headless monks, wheeling bats, and such delightful people as slink off Charles Addams' drawing board. But there is only one Northanger Abbey, and it has no existence in the modern world.

However, Preston Donner was continuing. "Surely you have heard of our local celebrity, Dr. Edward Austin?"

A hazy half-memory of a recent comment on the will of Dr. Austin, a monomaniacal collector of Austeniana, returned.

"But he's dead." I tried to recall a date and could not.

"Yes, he died five years ago—lived to be nearly a hundred. Miss Elizabeth, his eldest daughter, inherited the house for her lifetime. Unfortunately, the doctor's collection had absorbed most of his capital, even the fortune his wife had left him. And, by the terms of his will, nothing can be sold. It is a pity. His wife died over twenty years ago. She was Tessie Polchek, old Anton Polchek's daughter."

Another vague memory—steel—yes, one of those American success stories once so extolled, before it became a slightly shameful thing to work one's way up in the world by hard application to a job. Anton Polchek must have been one of the very last of the Alger heroes.

"—so Miss Elizabeth takes paying guests now." I must have missed a word or two. "This property belongs to her sister, Mrs. Emma Horvath. There is a garden walk uniting it to the Abbey."

The quaint term—again an echo of Aunt Otilda's world—"paying guest" riveted my attention. I had been in an inn room for a week, and I disliked inns, even when they were within walking distance of the library in which I had come to bury myself. I would be here for at least six weeks. What if—?

Taking courage, I mentioned my need. To my surprise, Preston Donner pounced upon my question eagerly. In fact, he was so interested I was flattered.

"How lucky! The large corner room is at present vacant. Perhaps I should explain that I am one of Miss Elizabeth's guests whenever I am in town. Having been a friend of the family for years, I was her first guest. It was my good fortune to be associated with Dr. Austin in the assembling of his collection. And that corner room is most suitable for a writer. It partly overlooks the garden and the quiet is most conducive to work, as I can testify." He might have been a rental agent, so did he extoll Northanger Abbey. There was a bus line offering only a ten-minute ride to the university and the library. Miss Elizabeth also provided breakfasts, and other meals if arrangements were made.

"Miss Elizabeth is home tonight," he ended. "If you wish I can escort you across the garden, save you the trouble of a second trip out."

He was moving too fast. I always react to pressure with the only defense I had learned during my Aunt Otilda years, digging in my heels and becoming evasive. Not that this had ever worked, and perhaps it would not now.

I wanted to discuss it with Theodosia, the only one here I could claim as more than a casual acquaintance. But she was now the center of a group deep in conversation. I did not have the courage to break into that.

Though I admit that the delights of the Abbey, as

Preston Donner recited them, attracted me (and I know there are some people who have a compulsion to settle matters neatly for their fellows), yet I did not want to be so summarily pushed. But he was already on his feet, and I did not again have the strength to say no.

Our leaving was not marked as we stepped out into moonlight. The sleet storm was over. Slush hardened on the ground, and our booted feet left misshapen tracks. In this light, the carriage house we had just left had some of the eerie, yet perilous, charm of a Rackham drawing.

"It is attractive," I commented.

My escort paused. "Yes. A pity things turned out the way they did. But Miss Emma will come to her senses. She must! She had the coach house converted for her nephew, the son of her sister Anne. Poor boy, he's in the Naval Hospital now—a returned prisoner of war from Vietnam. He was quite badly treated."

"But if it was a gift—" I was more intent in picking a cautious way over treacherous footing than I was in the information Preston Donner seemed so eager to supply.

"Unfortunately not a complete gift, though that was the understanding. Miss Emma had been unwell. She fell some months back and fractured her hip, which perhaps makes her so difficult to please. The Frimbees have a small child, and she thought that a child so close to her own dwelling bad for her nerves. She wanted only adults, so she offered a short lease to Mr. Cantrell. Then she had a sudden bad turn and now she is convalescing at Idleacres. Until she returns, nothing more can be decided. Irene and the child are living at the Abbey for the present."

This hint of family quarrels—nothing can be more vindictive or deadly—slowed my pace. I began to wish even more that I had never left Theodosia's hearthside. And I began to concoct, mentally, excuses to use once I reached the Abbey.

Our walk wound around the end of an untrimmed hedge into a frost-killed garden. There were clumps of trees and tall shrubs, and I caught a glimpse of a statue miserably cold in the moonlight. Beyond loomed the Abbey. Judging by a sky-outlined turret or two, it was certainly mock-gothic, perhaps of the worst General Grant period. In the dusk it repelled rather than charmed.

"It's big." To me it looked monstrous. There was only a faint glimmer of light in one or two widely separated windows.

"Ugly, too," he admitted promptly. "About the ugliest house in the county, which does give it distinction. Old Polchek had it built for his wife, then gave it to his daughter for a wedding present. Too bad for his granddaughters that he didn't have the foresight to tie up the funds in trust. Now it's just a white elephant poor Miss Elizabeth can't sell because of the will."

"The will?"

"All that is left of the capital is to provide additions to the library. That was Edward's dream. It doesn't matter to Miss Emma; she has life interest in Alexis Horvath's estate and her own money besides. And another daughter, Elinor, is dead. But Anne's a widow. Her husband went down with his ship during the war with Japan. She has only her pension. While Miss Elizabeth—" He slid his hand deftly under my arm in support as I slipped. "This is treacherous in this weather. I was not aware how much—"

I did not pull away from his touch, though I wanted to. Not because it was Preston Donner's hand, which was a firm support, but because—was I ever going to be allowed to forget? I called on the armor I had so harshly learned to wear.

Luckily the path now narrowed, so we had to go single file. With a murmur of excuse he went ahead. And he was not looking back when there was movement among the bushes to my left. Later, when it was to be very necessary for me to recall details of what— or what I thought—I had seen. I was not sure. How much was true, how much imagination?

I stopped so short I nearly slipped again as I sighted a figure between two overhanging shrubs. I gasped and it was gone, just as Preston Donner swung around. Luckily I had sense enough to edit my explanation, one of the few times in my life I thought fast.

"I thought I saw something moving—over there."

He peered along the line of my pointing finger.

"The bushes do assume odd shapes at night. I have noticed that myself."

But did any bush, no matter how large, I wondered, as I followed him on, ever assume the guise of a naval officer in full-dress, details of gold braid glinting in the moonlight? And particularly a naval officer in the type of uniform which had not been worn since the very early 1800s?

Either the Austins had some very lifelike and movable garden embellishments or—I suppressed my imagination with a heavy hand. On one small drink? No, I could *not* have seen that I thought I had.

2

Preston Donner turned into another walk, which brought us to an impressive portico. Inside the house, warmth enfolded us with that stuffy comfort promised by the late and very ugly Victorian solidity of such furnishing as could be seen.

The thick carpet did show some signs of wear, but what might have once been strident coloring now blended with oak paneling, which framed a wide marble staircase rising into shadows. If heat was abundant, the same was not true of light. The fixtures (including a marble goddess with a torch at the foot of the stair rail) were provided with bulbs of low wattage, which made little resistance to the general gloom.

"Who is there?" The call sounded from the cavern of a room to our right.

"Miss Elizabeth." Preston Donner came to attention. "It is I."

Though he motioned to me, I took time to shed boots, pull loose my headscarf. But, as I followed him, even the manners drilled into me by Aunt Otilda could not make me repress a startled gasp. If the hallway had been of the 1880s, this room underlined that promise with all of the period's unique hideousness.

There was an interference course of small tables, all crowded to the very edge with silver picture frames, china and glass. These elbowed velvet upholstered chairs, to form a near-impenetrable barrier between us and the woman seated beside a quite unnecessary blaze on the tiled hearth. All the clutter would have taken hours to catalog. I tried not to stare at such notable exhibits as a bunch of peacock feathers in a quite unbelievable vase—instead, I centered my attention on Miss Elizabeth Austin.

As the room, she was a period piece. Perhaps she was very near eighty. I would not have ventured to guess. But the age she chose to represent was the mature years of someone of a much earlier day. Her dress, the gored skirt of which brushed the toes of her velvet slippers, was black silk of a quality one no longer sees, meant to wear forever. Its vee-corsage was filled with a vestee of yellowed lace, supporting a high-boned collar to completely hide her throat. A garnet sunburst brooch weighted the lace, and more clusters of those dullish stones were set at her ears. Her silver hair puffed high under a visible net, leaving a soft fringe across her forehead. Recognition tugged at my memory: Queen Mary, just as she appeared in a recent biography's photographic illustration!

Mrs. Austin occupied her high-back chair with the erect and regal posture of royalty on display, graciously waiting for a lord chamberlain to present a visitor. Donner obliged her.

"Miss Elizabeth, this is Miss Erica Jansen. She is the author of—"

"Mistress of Melodrama." Miss Elizabeth gave a royal inclination of the head. "A most interesting book, Miss Jansen, if somewhat superficial. My dear mother was a friend of Mrs. Southworth's. At least you had the delicacy not to invent when you had no facts concerning some aspects of her personal life—a forebearance only too rare in so-called literary efforts these days."

She put out her hand. For an instant or two, the royal illusion held so strongly I felt inclined to make one of those quick up-and-down bobs one views upon such occasions in TV news. But when her fingers closed firmly about mine, the fantasy cracked and I was back in my own world.

"Miss Jansen is in Ladensville to do research at the university library," Preston Donner continued, as if etiquette denied me the right of stating anything for myself. "She mentioned a desire to move out of the inn."

Miss Elizabeth's lips firmed. I wondered if she disliked the suggestion which my escort had made, very much on his own authority.

"I spoke to her about the garden room," he continued, unabashed.

Miss Elizabeth regarded me measuringly. Oddly

enough, I, who had come here with the firm intention of not falling in with Donner's suggestion, now felt that to be accepted by Miss Elizabeth Austin as a paying guest was something of an accolade.

"Do you object to small children?" Her abrupt question was not what I had expected.

"I have not had much experience of them," I replied truthfully. I felt like a governess in one of those paperback gothics, being put searching questions concerning my fitness by a prospective employer. The setting was certainly correct. Even Miss Elizabeth fitted the proper pattern for such flights of fiction.

"You are forthright, Miss Jansen." Her small nod appeared to approve. "I ask because my niece and her son, a boy of three, are domiciled here for the present. When one is at work, sometimes extraneous noises are disturbing. My dear father always found them to be so. But this house is large, and you may not discover the situation troublesome. If you will follow me—"

She arose and glided—actually glided (an expression I had heretofore believed to be a cliché of second-rate novelists) to the door. Uncertainly, I followed.

Ascending the marble stairs with majestic unhaste, she brought me into a long hall better lighted than the one below. A door opened abruptly and a dumpy female, muffled in a threadbare flannel robe, head bristling with hair curlers, confronted us. If Miss Elizabeth fitted her surroundings to perfection, this apparition did not.

"Oh, it's you, Aunt." Her voice was flat, and her hand went up uncertainly to her curlers. This girl was very much an unsightly "before" in those "improve yourself" articles so beloved by magazines. Only she looked as if, in addition, she had no desire to proceed to the "after." Her eyes slid over me with no interest as she added:

"Stuart has a cold."

"Then call Dr. Bains, Irene. That is what physicians are for." Miss Elizabeth's reply was tinged with impatience. "Miss Jansen, my niece, Mrs. Frimsbee."

That untidy head nodded, but Mrs. Frimsbee's thoughts were plainly elsewhere. She stepped back and closed the door with some force as her aunt moved on to a farther chamber, switching on the light within.

The room was a large one, with flower-patterned drapes pulled across two sets of high windows. While the furniture was massive and of my grandmother's generation's taste, its ornate carving did not distract from a promise of comfort. And there was a hearth with wood ready laid for a fire. Indeed, the stolid look of it all held a promise of security. Suddenly I wanted just that.

"Would there be any objection to my typewriter, if I work at night?"

Her answer was a little out of character, for she rapped knuckles against the wall. "These are very thick. Sound does not carry unless one leaves the door open."

I was at a loss for what must follow. How does one discuss rates with a queen? Was this one of those refined guest houses I had read of (rather unbelievingly), where one puts one's rent in a neat envelope slipped under a doily on some hall table, to be collected unwitnessed later?

Once more Miss Elizabeth discarded her chosen role. She stated her rates with brisk firmness. So much for the room—two weeks in advance—with an extra fee for meals.

I found myself agreeing to move in the next day. The belief that I was being honored by admittance to the Abbey was not only rooted in my landlady's air, but by Preston Donner's congratulations when I rejoined him in the hall below.

As I was putting on my boots, Mrs. Frimsbee came clumping down. Her flannel robe had been replaced by an all-duty coat of unbecoming black and white plaid, and she adjusted its shoulder hood as she descended.

"I'll be back as soon as I can, Aunt. Dr. Bains says to use the vaporizer and I'm all out of fluid—"

"It's a bad night out, Miss Irene," Preston Donner said quickly. "Let me do your errand."

Her sullenly tired expression did not lighten. There was no change in the droop of her mouth. "It's Vita-Flow. And you'd better get the large size. Have Mr. Ferely put it on my account." Without a word of thanks, she turned to the stairs and went back with the same heavy-footed tread.

Preston Donner was plainly torn between two acts of courtesy, and I made the decision for him.

"You go to the drugstore, Mr. Donner. The walk to the carriage house is plain. I couldn't possibly lose my way."

But when outside we separated, and that shadow-filled garden lay once more before me, I rather regretted my helpfulness. There was what I had seen—I could swear I had *not* imagined it. Now I struck out at as brisk a pace as the footing would allow. Cold nipped, and snow had begun to fall. Why had I taken a room at the Abbey? The first thing I must do upon my return to the inn was to cancel the whole thing.

I had been watching the fast-filling tracks we had left, and was suddenly aware there was a third set of prints. The small heel, the narrow toe, could only have been left by a woman.

They had appeared from around a bush, neither from the house or the carriage house, as far as I could tell. Had it not been so dark I might have backtracked a little, for my curiosity was aroused. But the dense shrubbery fed unpleasant suggestions to my imagination and I hurried on.

Under the bench in the carriage-house foyer was a collection of boots and overshoes. Ruling out the strictly masculine, and the broader soled footgear such as my own, there were three pair which might have left those prints. I ran an exploring finger over the toe of each and the last was wet. I was almost sure that Theodosia had worn a similar pair when I had met her at the library. But short of playing Cinderella's prince and trying them on the company, I would never know. After all, what did it matter?

"Erica!" Theodosia stood looking at me in surprise. "Where have you been?"

I started. "Mr Donner suggested I see about a room at the Abbey. I do want to get out of that inn."

She laughed. "I might have known Preston would be drumming up trade for his precious Miss Elizabeth. Where is he now—lurking outside, afraid to face me for trying to plant you in that Victorian horror house? To him, Miss Elizabeth is a period piece to be carefully preserved. But he needn't have recruited you, though I'll admit your room would be comfortable, and she does have an excellent cook. Don't take me seriously if you are really interested. Just to rent a room there would not mean that you would be pulled into anything."

"What do you mean?"

"Austin family affairs. Unfortunately, we were dragged in through Mrs. Horvath. But their troubles are none of yours. I've nothing against Miss Elizabeth. In a way she's a grand relic, a monument if you like. She's taken enough blows to floor an elephant, but no one has heard her complain."

"Maybe this is too far uptown." I mustered one of the arguments which had occurred to me during my return across the garden.

Only Theodosia now made an about-face. She dropped her banter and spoke soberly:

"My girl, if you can stand living in that house with the Austins—and a very muddled lot they are, as I will tell you when we have more time—I shall welcome your being here. I have an idea, which I trust is only the fruit of my imagination, that something unpleasant is building. Now, if that frightens you away, I shan't be surprised.

"As for transportation, don't give it a thought. We can keep working hours together. Which, goodness knows, I must do now. Plunge into serious reading. It keeps one from thinking all the time. I sometimes believe that more than just Emma Horvath's spite haunts this place. Which gives me another idea—"

But what that might be I was not to learn as she was hailed from the other room and, with a small gesture of annoyance, she disappeared.

I returned to the party, wondering if I had been missed. I need not have flattered myself. Leslie Lowndes was across the room, and I was drawn into a comfortable clique grouped about a moon-faced lady who wrote cookbooks and was having a passionate conversation with a recently returned foreign correspondent about the proper use of preserved ginger. Since the argument involved references to geography, history, literature, and important personalities, I had my horizons rapidly expanded and enjoyed every moment of it.

The foreign correspondent even escorted me back to the inn, and I was complacently aware the my evening had been a success. I was right. Ladensville might not have changed much, but I had. I did not need to fear the past.

As I gathered my key from the desk, I had the second shock of the evening. Though it was now after midnight, there were people in the bar. I sighted one and fled into the hall beyond, with the same instinct for self-preservation which makes any small, hunted thing crouch into immobility, frozen with fear.

That recognition wiped away all my confidence and content. For one ghastly moment I was afraid I was going to be physically sick. Ever since I had made my decision to come here, I had debated the possibility of such an encounter. But I had thought it reasonably remote. Nothing could really bring Mark Rohmer back into my life again.

What does one do when the painful past perches on a barstool and you see it without warning? Only, and I clung to that, I had not *met* him; I had seen him in time and was safe. Consoling myself so, I groped my way down the hall, feeling if I turned my head I might well see him striding behind. Which was sheer nonsense. Long since he must have forgotten my very existence. Or if he did recall me—what amusement I must have afforded him!

In my room, the door locked, my common sense resumed full control. What if I had seen Mark? There was no earthly reason why our paths should cross. But what if he were staying *here*?

Like a sleepwalker, I brought out my suitcase and began to pack. Was I really sure it *was* Mark at all? There had been a time when the right tilt of a dark head, the set of erect shoulders, a swing of step, had all misled me into false recognitions.

I dropped down on the bed. I had thought I was cured. Did coming back mean this again? Tomorrow—tomorrow I would be in Northanger Abbey—so far removed from anything which coud remind me of the past that I would dare to relax. Better a house with a smoldering family feud than a major in an inn.

Though I went wearily to bed, I could not sleep. For when I closed my eyes, or even opened them again upon the impersonal darkness of the room, it was summer, not late fall. Summer hot and humid as only Maryland summers could be.

Summer—no, not the whole summer, just six weeks

in truth—yet those stretched and stretched into a whole season. Six weeks from the morning in the college cafeteria when Mark Rohmer had sat down beside me at the table shared by the project people. Mark Rohmer, who led all the secretaries to reach for their compacts, who had caused even staid Miss Hawes to observe in a wintery tone that it was an excellent thing for our combined labors that all Major Rohmer's assistants were of the male sex.

Not only was he handsome, but he had the added attraction of the exotic, his background forming an item of conversation. Since the consciousness of racial beginnings had become so important, a Blackfoot Indian, the first of his race to graduate from West Point, was doubly notable. To this he could add a dominant personality and a high degree of trained intelligence.

One did not, in the very prejudice-conscious Sixties, cling to the old mental picture of feathered warbonnet and facial paint, no matter how much one had been conditioned by film and book in childhood. On the other hand, neither did one quite imagine a cultivated man of the world (I had been used at that time to only Aunt Otilda's beliefs and turns of speech) to be an Indian.

On that momentous morning of our meeting, I had frozen as I had always done on the very rare occasions I had met an attractive man. My Aunt Otilda had early conditioned me to accept the fact I was without any pretense to attractiveness, and unredeemably shy and gauche into the bargain. But for some reasons, Major Rohmer had not acted as if I were invisible. On the contrary, he had persisted with various conversational openings until I dared to thaw a little. He must have considered me a challenge of sorts. Perhaps the game he then proceeded to play was born of boredom at being in Ladensville when all his desires lay elsewhere. At the time I began to believe that we had many likes and dislikes in common.

Acquaintance, on my part, grew to something else. Thinking about it even now, years later, could bring a burning flush to my face. Why spare myself? I had been a far too naïve and silly fool! I should have anticipated the end.

There had been the Saturday when we had both been free for the afternoon, and he had asked me to lunch at a country inn. I had been nearly shaking with excitement—and—any—no! We had gone across the road after eating to where there was a church bazaar in progress. He had won a horrible rayon bedspread at a raffle and had laughingly given it back to be reoffered. There had been such good times—when his very company had released me from the hard shell of self-doubt my childhood had encased about me. If I could only remember those and forget the rest!

Six weeks of excitement, dreams, hopes—then his going. But letters—letters I fed fiercely to a fire five months later, as fast as I could. There had been a last letter to bring me to Washington.

Now my hands balled into fists. Go on—remember this—relive it—don't try to dress it up, excuse your own stupid hopes for the impossible. I was so humiliated to think of what I had believed might be possible that thereafter my only relief was that Aunt Otilda never knew. If she had, I would never have been able to survive the constant carping into which she had lapsed during the last two years of her narrow and self-imprisoned life.

The message awaiting me at the hotel desk—Major Rohmer would be detained—he would call after six. Four hours to kill, and I could not spend them in my room staring at the wall. I was restless, needing to walk off the excitement which invigorated me. Down the avenue—the purchase of a scarf. (I burned that along with the letters, a sorry waste, my prudent training argued at the time—but I could not look at it except with dull sickness.) Then, I was turning into that other hotel because Sally Logan had said they had such a superlative buffet luncheon. That had been an adventure; super hotels were not my usual style, but that day I felt so liberated I dared it.

Then—in the lobby seeing him—and her. She was, like Leslie Lowndes, everything I was not. The latest hairstyle, the perfect-featured face, the drawling voice which caressed languidly, clothes I could never hope to acquire. A hand with an emerald ring laid in obvious possession on Mark's arm, eyes for no one but him. Then the voice of the deferential hotel clerk, pitched—perhaps—no, not just perhaps, but necessarily, high to reach me:

"Mrs. Rohmer, there is a message for you."

Even as she half-turned to pick up the envelope he held out, she had not released that proprietary grasp on Mark. And—

Now I sat up in bed, dug my fists down on either side of me.

Remember—remember—you asked for it.

Mark's eyes flitting around over her shoulder as she busied herself with that envelope. Meeting mine. Nothing—nothing at all in his face. It was as blank as a stranger's. What my features must have expressed at that moment, I do not even dare to guess.

Somehow I turned—I was out in the street, thrusting through sidewalk traffic, before I was thinking straight again. Girlfriend and wife—I know that my reaction would be considered weird in these days of permissiveness. I can only offer that I was reared, and so imbued, by a stern set of moralistic rules that I found the situation not amusing—as it would be to my contemporaries—but soiling. Open marriages and meaningful encounters—I read about them, I touched upon them in the persons of some of my acquaintances, but that mode of life is totally foreign to me.

It had taken me very little time to check out of my hotel, find that there was a flight out, which I could just make after a mad dash to the airport. I sat crouched in my seat, sick and shaking, knowing that I had never been anything at all but perhaps a source of mild amusement.

For days after I cringed every time the phone rang, made an effort to sort the mail before Aunt Otilda (no matter to whom a letter was addressed, its contents must be shared in *her* house) could sight it. It took me a week at least back home before I realized with great thankfulness of heart that it could well be Major Rohmer did not know my address. Though why I expected to hear from him I cannot answer. His blank face in the lobby had been answer enough. If he had put himself to the "give the poor girl a thrill" bit, he had succeeded admirably. Having achieved that, I should be thankful that fate had taken me to that point of contact.

Yes, I had gone to Washington, my nerve stiffened to the point of perhaps playing the very role which, after, disgusted me. What would I have done, in my euphoria, if Mark had suggested a togetherness weekend? Luckily, I never had to learn the depths of my infatuation.

No one had ever known back home. I had found it very easy to lapse into what Aunt Otilda expected of me, making no more gestures towards any kind of freedom. There was a soothing security to living by her rules. When she died at last, I found myself mistress of a small income, a house I speedily sold, and then a studio apartment, and a chance to see if there was anyone under my skin except Miss Jansen's niece: the one who works in the library, you know—a very dull girl—but well meaning.

I had come again to Ladensville, mainly because the library of the university contained two collections of books and manuscripts needed in my present research. Or—or was it because some unregenerate part of me had—

Setting my teeth, I settled my head once more on my pillow, with an emphatic thump. I was older, and, I hoped, wiser. Maybe I was an anachronism in my generation, but then I had never felt any kinship with people of my own age. What had a psychotherapist friend of mine (who had once tried to get me to sort out my badly confused inner self) said? Children were programmed from birth and it was the hardest thing in the world to reprogram them. Each must want to be another person with all his or her heart and soul.

I was satisfied—I had to be—with the Erica Jansen I was. With that Erica, I felt as safe as a hunted animal deep in some warm hole. As long as I did not try to venture forth, but just turned around and around where I was, then I thought—I knew—I could bear waking up each morning to face life, dark and colorless though it might seem to others.

But what had brought Mark Rohmer to Ladensville again?

I wrenched my thoughts, fought them. Tomorrow it will not matter at all. You'll be firmly settled in that bastion of propriety, in Miss Elizabeth's house. Holding to that, I somehow did achieve a measure of dream-haunted and unrefreshing sleep.

3

I was out of the inn before breakfast the next morning, scuttling off in a way I knew was a disgrace to my self-respect, restraining my inclination to keep looking over my shoulder only by stern effort. If I expected Mark Rohmer to rise up between me and the outer door, I was disappointed. Though in punishment for my foolishness I shivered enough while waiting for the reluctant arrival of the taxi.

In the daylight, the Abbey held no mystery at all. The bushes, which last night had appeared only screens to hide what writers of horror tales (who have flogged their imaginations into utter fatigue) call "the unmentionable," were only shrubs, sadly weighted now with soft snow. When I was deposited with suitcase and flight bag at the door, my main thought was of hunger, though to expect breakfast waiting would be too much. I could stop at the coffee shop later.

My chilled finger punched the bell button with perhaps too much vigor. But I was eager to get under cover, and I begrudged the moments there on the doorstep, as a chill wind curled around me. At last the door opened with a decided creak, and I found myself facing a dried wisp of a woman. In her youth she must have been as tall as Miss Elizabeth Austin, but age, and perhaps years of labor, had bowed her forward, hunching her thin shoulders. Her hair was a frizz of gray and black, the most of it pinned up under a cap, while her black dress was covered with a bib apron. Through granny glasses (which were no affectation of the moment's fashion but really of another time) she peered at me. And there was no welcome in her face. I found myself a little at a loss, facing that hostile stare.

"I'm Miss Jansen. Miss Elizabeth rented me a room last night—" I fought to sound not apologetic, as if I were pleading for shelter.

She made no answer save a duck of her head as she pulled the heavy door farther open to let me clump in, bags in hand. I was feeling that I must cease to drip on the carpet as soon as possible. I shed my boots with all the speed I could muster while the woman stooped and picked up, before I could stop her, my baggage. She went on to climb the stair slowly, as if the ascent tried aching joints, while I hurried to join her.

Once more we paced down the upper hall and I was finally installed in the same room Miss Elizabeth had shown me last night. As the elderly maid put down my luggage, she fumbled in the pocket of her apron and withdrew a slip of paper which she held out to me before turning to go out the door.

I unfolded the piece, plain torn from a phone tablet, and read:

"Please call—564-2201—Theodosia."

"Please." I raised my voice before my guide disappeared entirely. "Where is the phone?"

She halted, did not turn, but looked back at me over one hunched shoulder.

"Back hall—miss—" Her words grated out of her as if she resented spending any of them.

Her far-from-welcoming attitude was daunting. I eyed my suitcase dubiously as she left. It seemed at that moment I had been far too hasty in coming here. Theodosia—perhaps I should have talked things over with someone better able than Preston Donner to share facts. I left my things packed, wondering how I could gracefully undo what my lack of thought had gotten me into, as I went prospecting for the phone.

It was in the back hall, right enough, and Theodosia might have been hovering about the other end of the line waiting for me, so prompt was her answer at the first ring.

"Erica?" Her voice was very hurried, a tone of— desperation? No, I was imagining things again—in it. "Are you committed to anything today or tomorrow?"

I was surprised, snapped out of my own preoccupation.

"Just to breakfast, then a prowl through my notebooks." I tried to be light in touch, meet the standard I believed Theodosia's intimates would use.

I heard her laugh. "Breakfast? You can have that

here, and I have a suggestion to make. Come on, right away!" Once more that faintly breathless tinge crept into her speech. And she hung up apparently with no doubt that I would indeed obey her summons.

However, I wanted to. It would give me time to think—or at least to learn from her a little more about the Austins and what I might have ignorantly stepped into. As I turned from the phone, the silence of the house closed in about me in an odd fashion. Even in daylight, these halls were dim. Through a partly open door to my right I caught sight of a half-cleared table, crumpled napkins, a stray spoon lying here and there. The light was grayish without a hint of sun. All the rest of the doors were firmly closed in what seemed a secretive fashion. At that moment the sensation of intruding was very strong. I was deeply sorry I had allowed my stupid involvement with the past to stampede me into coming here.

Pulling on my boots, I went out once more, standing under the portico to look around and make sure of my path. The snow had hidden the walk down which I had come last night, but I do have a sense of direction, and I was quite sure, in spite of the screens of high-growing bushes and trees, where it ran. Underfoot the snow was near-slush, and my tracks were the first to mark it.

Perhaps the garden had once been a formal one. There were benches, now pillowed with snow, and a statue or two to be seen. To my left, as I swung into the way leading to the carriage house, there was a far thicker growth. Still I caught sight of a roof out in that direction, or the portion of one, which was large enough to suggest it covered a building bigger than any modern garage or perhaps even the converted carriage house towards which I was now bound.

It took me only a few minutes to get around to the scarlet door marking Theodosia's domain. Again, she might have been waiting, for I had no more than let the knocker fall than she opened to me.

"Erica, come in!" She reached out and caught at my arm to draw me towards her. I was a little disconcerted at her action. I liked her, admired her, but I had not considered that I had any right to claim close friendship with her. My upbringing had effectively smothered my own spontaneous reaction to anyone. Aunt Otilda had had a horror of what she referred to as "indiscriminate acquaintanceships," and had fastidiously weaned me early from casual friendships—and kept me religiously from close ones. I found it extremely difficult now to let down any barriers, even in the most fleeting of contacts.

Even inside, Theodosia did not loosen that hold on me, but I was propelled to a small breakfast room. My discarded coat, with its attached hood, was taken, to be flung over a neighboring chair, while my hostess had a mug of coffee to my hand before I had a chance to think.

"Listen." Theodosia assembled a plate of scrambled eggs taken from a covered heating pan, inserted bread into a toaster, and then seated herself across from me, pushing salt and pepper nearer. "I've got myself into something."

She did not look directly at me, but fiddled with a pot of marmalade, pushing it out and then drawing it back again. "You know, I'm working on the old Kitteridge case. It has all the elements of the wildest melodrama. And there's good chance of it going not only for a book, but for a TV special. God knows we need the advance and that sale, if Lottie can make it for us. She phoned yesterday, before the party, and my deadline is advanced if I want the TV chance. Two months ago I tried to get an interview with the lawyer who handles what is left of the Kitteridge property. I need to see the house, naturally—the geography of the place is a part of the general story. He has been stalling, then this morning, at the crack of dawn practically, I get a call that he is going on a trip of inspection there and will clear it for me to take a look around.

"It's a hundred miles from here, and in this kind of weather I'm not going to try to make a round trip in one day. I couldn't, anyway, and see all I want to. Gordon is tied up, and the fact is I don't like traveling alone. Would you be willing to tag along? It would be for two, maybe three, days; and, after all, the whole story is in your period, too. It's a chance to see the place and I don't think anyone has for years, unless this Johnson trots out there by himself from time to time."

I felt as if I had been handed the trip to England I had always longed for. The Kitteridge legend of family disgrace, murder, and mystery was known to me, yes. And to see the actual site, with Theodosia who was writing about it, was a chance I could hardly believe I would ever have.

"Oh—yes—!"

I made a hurried breakfast, dashed back to cram what might be needed for a short trip into my ever-expandable flight bag, and was ready for Theodosia before an hour had passed, leaving a note for Miss Elizabeth, whom I had yet to see, enclosing the promised prepaid rent and explaining my absence.

We did have three days, exciting for both of us. It was on the way back that Theodosia spoke abruptly.

"I hate to go back. There's something about that place which seems wrong."

That she spoke of the carriage house, I understood. But her words also evoked for me the Abbey, and I, too, experienced a reluctance. It was now as if I returned from a vacation into bondage, the same slightly shrinking feeling I had always had before the life Aunt Otilda decreed had again closed about me after some very brief escape.

"The Austins—at least Miss Elizabeth—" I ventured, "almost seem as if they were living in another age."

"They are. Time stopped for them at least fifty years ago!" she flashed back. "I gather that the old boy, Dr. Edward, was one of those domestic tyrants such as stud Victorian novels and give satisfaction to modern researchers. He married beneath him, according to the canons of his clan and time, when he married old Polchek's daughter. And I gather he never let her forget it. There were four daughters, no sons.

"Elizabeth was the oldest, then there was Elinor born a good ten years later, Emma, two years younger, and finally Anne. Elinor was the black sheep. She was crossed out of the family Bible when she eloped with Harlan Blackmur."

"Eloped?" I tried to connect such an exploit with

the grim, time-embedded luxury of the Abbey. Yes, an elopement might even figure there.

"It was because of the theater," Theodosia continued. "Edward was completely immersed in his Austeniana research. He spent most of Tillie's cash on that. Finally young Blackmur—he was acting as Edward's secretary at the time—suggested a theater to give plays made from the novels. Somehow he awakened a spark in Dr. Edward, and almost overnight the carriage house was enlarged, turned into a little theater, with Blackmur in charge. He had had some stage experience, and from all I have heard he was a charmer. Perhaps he thought he could manage the old man after he got the theater. They gave just one play, made from *Pride and Prejudice*. Then Elinor and he were caught publicly in an unmistakably intimate scene of their own. There were more fireworks than the start of World War II, and Elinor and Blackmur were shown the gate—fast.

"It was made very clear that Dr. Edward did not intend to welcome any suitors. It might mean that some of Tillie's lovely money would be diverted from his own beloved pursuit. Tillie, I gather, was thoroughly crushed by that time. Her father had brought her up in the woman-is-property-and-a-servant belief, from his European background, and she just never had a chance to exert herself.

"Emma escaped by charming Horvath—he was younger than Dr. Edward but not much. And he was rich. She saw that he was about the only escape she would ever get when she met him at her grandfather's house. I think he fancied Tillie at one time, before the old man thought Dr. Edward's social connections might mean a step up for his daughter. So she had her wedding big enough to plaster all the newspapers before, during, and after. She traveled in Europe, after Horvath conveniently died, and she cut quite a swath there as one of the semi-Jet Set. Then, when she began to age she could not stand losing any sign of youth among them, and came back here to play great lady frog in the small puddle of Ladensville.

"Anne got herself a man, too. Through Emma, really—an attaché, naval—at one of the smaller embassies. She and Emma were fairly close. They had the same outlook on things. Captain Frimsbee rose in rank, due to the attrition of the war, and went down with his ship in late '44. Now Anne pushes along on her pension and spends her life trading on naval connections for long visits. She makes herself useful to such hostesses as will give her room and board, while Emma, finding Anne's connections no longer of any great use, has written her off. Emma did fix up the carriage house and present it to Anne's son, who was a naval officer and a good escort now and then. But when he married and then was invalided out of the picture in Vietnam, she speedily decided that Irene and son were no longer necessary. Irene does tend to be a dreary soul, and Emma, as I hear it, dislikes any suggestion of ill health or trouble about her.

"Poor Miss Elizabeth was the one who was caught. Her mother was an invalid—real or imaginary—for a good many years. I would think that any wife of Dr. Edward might well take to her bed to escape. And during those years, she ran the house. Not only that but she found her own fanciful retreat. Deliberately or not, she became a period piece, out of a much earlier period. I think she really picked the year of her birth—1899—and decided to stay in it as either her mother or her grandmother. She does it magnificently and has become a kind of timeless symbol of another age."

"Why, I wonder?" Another kind of retreat? Did Miss Elizabeth feel secure only wrapped in the trappings of an era where there was a certain solidity to life which we had never known and could probably never know in the future either? We speak of that immediate past now with sneers, with stimulated horror at its narrowness. Still, those contemporary with it were the last to see life as a solid and firm thing. For the persons who abided by its rites and customs, there had been that security.

"Miss Elizabeth is probably the only one who knows. If she is happier playing that role, then she deserves to be allowed to do so. She certainly has little in the modern day to make her even passably content. Dr. Edward kept his grip on Tillie's money even from the grave. He set up a trust fund to buy future relics—if any could be found—for his proposed Austin library. Miss Elizabeth got the house—period. That she has managed to keep going at all is a tribute to her grit and drive. If she can save pennies wearing out her mother's old frocks—such as she considers suitable—then she will do it. Every cent counts to her, nowadays. I think Emma makes her a small allowance—and expects a big return in service for it."

"Emma does not sound like a very pleasant neighbor—"

"She's a rich bitch!" Theodosia spat. "She has abominable manners, the cunning of a peasant without any real intelligence, and the instincts of a Nazi storm trooper. Two months ago she broke her hip and since then she has—luckily—been removed from our horizon. *I* intend to remove myself before she comes out and back from that superlative nursing home and takes up residence again." Theodosia spoke with such heat, I could well believe that she had met Emma Horvath head-on in some contest of wills, but she did not enlarge on that last statement.

However, as we swept up the now-cleared drive leading to Northanger Abbey, I was very much of a mind to move myself as soon as I could locate another place. Nothing Theodosia had told me made the future look pleasant. As we pulled in to stop under the portico, Theodosia exclaimed and pointed.

Against the massive front door, there hung a spray of evergreen tied with a swag of deep purple ribbon. I blinked. Again time rolled away—the custom of another age confronted us.

"Who—" Theodosia wondered.

I was reluctant to raise my hand to the bell near that antiquated sign of dignified and decorous grief. Before I could force myself to that move, the door itself opened, and Preston Donner came out.

"Miss Jansen—Mrs. Cantrell—" He made his funny, old-fashioned inclination of the head as if he, too, had somehow been touched by the formal air of the past. "Mrs. Horvath is dead." He spoke abruptly, almost as if he held us somehow to blame for that. I would have expected him to use the usual euphemism of "passed away"—his bald words were out of the character I had built for him.

"When?" Theodosia asked, as he added nothing to that.

"Monday night. The funeral is tomorrow. It is very hard on Miss Elizabeth. If you will excuse me—I have an errand—" His briskness was almost rude as he turned away. I wondered if he indeed felt some emotion.

Theodosia looked at me. "If you can't stick it here," she said quickly, "our latchstring is out. Just come over."

I thanked her quickly. But I did not intend to become a problem for the Cantrells, even though I might well discover it best to leave Northanger Abbey.

Inside I fronted Miss Elizabeth herself. As I could have expected, her floor-sweeping dress was black. Above the high collar of that, her face was white, her skin looked like well-worn, grayish parchment, drawn tightly over the good bones. Ill at ease, I muttered condolences, the usual meaningless things one says at such times. Only, looking at Miss Elizabeth, I wished that there *was* something I could do for her.

She made a visible effort to retain her usual composure. "Thank you." Her voice was very remote and cool. "Everything has been arranged. Though I fear we are not serving dinner this evening—"

"Of course. And perhaps I should arrange other accommodations—"

"Not at all, Miss Jansen." Her voice firmed. "The

service will be held here, since my sister will rest in our private lot. But the ceremony is only for the immediate family. I appreciate your thoughtfulness."

I felt a twinge of shame, for my proposed flight had been really for my benefit, not hers. And by Theodosia's account, she needed money.

"Of course you are free to leave—" Did her eyes hold a shadow of a plea? I decided quickly that that was only fancy. But I was forced into a decided denial.

She followed me up the stairs apparently on some errand of her own. I jerked open the door of my room. Another door down the hall matched mine in a second creak. Irene came out. She was not wearing a dingy robe this time, but a trim black suit—though that, on her, accented just those points of figure better concealed. Her mousy blond hair had been pinned up and lavish makeup (especially blue eye shadow) applied with not the most fortunate results.

Sighting Miss Elizabeth she paused, her too-red lips pulled into a wry grimace. Aunt and niece-by-marriage, they might have been defending rival barricades. Miss Austin lobbed the first grenade.

"You are going out, Irene? I thought that Stuart—"

Irene interrupted, her voice shrill. "Maud promised to sit with him."

"Maud was to have the afternoon off. Tomorrow—"

"I know very well what will happen tomorrow, Aunt. In the meantime I have important business of my own!"

"I did not know that the hospital had extra visiting hours—"

Irene Frimsbee scowled defiantly. "I'm not going to

the hospital." She shaped each word distinctly, as one might to a child or a deaf person. "And I'm paying Maud for her time. She's satisfied."

She brought her right hand from behind her back. In it was a clutch purse of black, a gaudy rhinestone "I" on it. Her banner of revolt so displayed, she faced Miss Elizabeth. I guessed her defiance was shaky.

"I can't help it!" She protested in answer to something which had not been spoken. "I can't pretend I'm sorry she's gone. You can't expect me to, knowing what she did!"

"I expect nothing, Irene." Miss Elizabeth's voice was even more remote.

Irene Frimsbee pushed past to the stairs. I was suddenly conscious I had been a witness to a scene which did not concern me, and hurriedly shut my door.

The next hour I spent unpacking and inspecting my room. But I was haunted by the feeling I should be doing just the opposite. At last I dropped into a chair by the window. The winter dusk had already begun to close in, and I could see the wink of car lights along the street.

A small foreign car swung into the drive. It did not disappear under the portico but passed on. I was curious enough to go to watch it through the garden window. A man had gotten out, was talking to someone still within, as if he were loath to go. Then he started down the walk leading to the carriage house. Gordon Cantrell—

My watch told me it was a little past five, not too early to hunt a restaurant. But I was to witness a second burst of family fireworks before I left. As I was putting on my boots in the lower hall there was a steady peal of the doorbell. Being closest, I automatically answered.

A taxi was pulling away, while outside stood a woman muffled in a fur coat, smart but scuffed luggage piled to one side. She stared at me appraisingly.

"And who might you be?" she demanded abruptly.

"Erica Jansen." I was startled into answering before her rudeness awakened my resentment.

Just as I had been attracted to Miss Elizabeth at our first meeting, so was I repelled by this newcomer. She crossed the threshold and looked about the hall peevishly, making no move to bring in her luggage. Since I certainly did not intend to do so, and the wind was cold, I closed the door.

"Anne!" Miss Elizabeth appeared from the back of the house, holding out her hands in welcome. But Anne Frimsbee ignored her gesture. Instead, she eyed the closed door of the parlor.

"So she's dead at last." There was no mistaking a satisfied note in that.

"Anne!" Miss Elizabeth repeated in shocked reproof.

Anne Frimsbee rounded on her elder sister. "You don't expect me to shed tears—not after the way she's treated Charles. She was as money-mean as they come. And you know as well as I do that's true. My bags are out there—I've had a hellish trip, and I'm going to rest until dinner." She mounted the stairs without looking back.

Miss Elizabeth sighted me. If she was disturbed at a witness, she did not show it.

"You are going out, Miss Jansen?" Was that a quiet hint that the sooner I took myself off the better?

"For dinner." I was eager to be away. "Is there a restaurant within walking distance, Miss Austin? I would like to be back early."

"There is a McDonald's two blocks over. Or the Humbolt. That is one block west and three down. Mr. Donner is fond of that. Oh," she said as I opened the door, "there is Anne's luggage."

Since Miss Elizabeth was moving forward as if to collect the bags, I did what I would not have done for their owner—I handed them within. But after the door closed, I was glad to be out. The warm comfort and security the house had seemed to offer at first was near gone. I spattered through slush and glanced aloft at massing clouds. I must make up my mind and move, as soon as I decently could.

When I entered the Humbolt, I was glad of my choice. It looked as if it had been remodeled from an old barn, and because I was early I had a good choice of tables. My selection was a booth to one side, out of the line of any draft from the doors.

The prices quoted on the menu were high, but I thought I deserved a treat. Only when I had given my order did I hear the murmur of voices from the booth ahead of mine.

"—dead. You'll have to do something—" Low and masculine.

"Just give me time. I have a plan. Just you be at—" a feminine voice arose and then dropped again.

The waiter brought me salad, then the party before me hailed him. I would not have seen the speakers, had not my napkin slipped to the floor. As I made a grab for it I caught sight of a coat which could not easily be forgotten. That hideous black and white plaid was the one Irene Frimsbee had worn Saturday night.

So Irene had a meeting here with a man whom I had not seen. The "death"—Mrs. Horvath's?

I lingered as long as I could, for I disliked the prospect of the cold walk back. But most of all, though there was no real reason for that, I dreaded to return to that house. Only I would not intrude on Theodosia in spite of her invitation.

Marriage—what led people to marry then find themselves duped? Did Theodosia regret hers? It was simply that I sensed hers was not an easy household. Even I might have faced such a situation had—that thought I determinedly pushed away.

It was only seven, but I had plenty to read and a good lamp in my room. So I plowed back once more through the slush. Coming in from the cold, I was aware of a cloying odor of flowers—and glanced apprehensively at the closed doors of the parlor. No funeral home for the Austins—Miss Elizabeth was keeping to the once well-known pattern of a lying-in-state. But the problems of the family were not mine.

When I reached my room, sleet beat against the window. I looked over my books, but I could not settle down to research reading tonight. On the drum table near the fireplace was what I should have expected to find in this house: a full set of Jane Austen's ironical romances.

Emma, so esteemed by many critics, was never to my taste. *Pride and Prejudice* I knew too well for it to hold me when I was disturbed. My hand hovered between the glorious fun of *Northanger Abbey* and the quieter *Persuasion*. It was Anne Elliot's renunciation, and the ten-year-after satisfying reward, which I chose. Those passing years—I was *not* going to think of my hopeless five. I opened the book:

Sir Walter Elliot, of Kellynch-hall, in Somersetshire, was a man who, for his own amusement, never took up any book but the Baronetage—

The familiar magic held. I read on, forgetting my uneasy qualms. But before I went to bed I left the hall door slightly ajar. Having been reared in a houschold where bedrooms were seldom closed, I found it claustrophobia to be shut in.

There was a dim radiance in the hall from the head of the stairs, but most of the corridor was dark. I drifted into that hazy state which is neither sleep nor full consciousness. Then, I do not know how much later, I was sitting up in bed, my covers clutched to me, straining my ears for a repetition of that sound which had jolted me into heart-hammering wakefulness.

4

I pulled my robe about me and went to the door of my room. Peering out warily, I could see the faint glow of light from the stairwell. Between that and me were blots formed by two chairs back to the wall. Had a phone ring, sounding through the quiet house, awakened me? Or the closing of a door, the murmur of a voice?

Shivering, I stood listening. The silence was a little frightening. I could not guess how late it was—my watch lay on the bedside table behind me. All the doors along the hall were closed. This was like being left alone in an empty house—no, not an *empty* house—rather, one inhabited by someone, or something, I would rather not meet. My hand was on the

knob of my own door, ready to close it against that
silence which lay like a breath between two sighs.

Footsteps on the stairs—but with an oddly long
pause between each. Against my will, I was drawn
down the shadowed corridor to the head of the stair-
way. Shock pushed me into quick action.

Miss Elizabeth was dragging herself up, plainly by
great effort. Both her hands pulled at the rail. Her
body sagged as if only a determined will kept her on
her feet at all.

She did not speak as I reached her. Only she turned
her head, so even in this faint light, I saw a face which
might be the death mask of the self-confident woman I
knew. Fear chilled me even as I managed to half-sup-
port her up the last few steps. Once on the level floor
of the hall, she swayed and might have fallen had I not
taken a good portion of her weight.

"Room—" Her voice was a husky whisper. "Last
room—"

Somehow she stayed on her feet, kept moving, as I
steered her to the last door along the corridor. Doctor?
I must get a doctor! Mrs. Anne Frimsbee—any
help—I glanced at each door we passed, wishing I
knew on which to knock.

Our wavering progress halted. Miss Elizabeth
fumbled with a small, jet-beaded purse clipped to her
belt. Her shaking fingers could not master the catch
and I caught her murmur. "Key—"

I found the key while she leaned against the wall,
her breath coming in heavy gasps as if she could not
get enough air into her laboring luungs. The lock

clicked and I groped along the wall within to locate the light switch.

Miss Elizabeth eluded my grasp and tottered ahead, to fall, rather than seat herself, in a rocking chair. Under the light, her haggard face had such a ghastly color my alarm grew. Was she going to die, perhaps of a heart attack, before I could get help? Yet dared I leave her to summon that? Irene's room was the only one I was certain of, and I was about to go for her when Miss Elizabeth sat up a little straighter.

Perhaps reaching the sanctuary of her own room worked as a restorative. Although she still rested her head against the comb back of the chair, a faint color was back in her gray-white cheeks. Now I dared to pick up one of her paper-white, blue-veined hands, enclosing the cold and clammy flesh between my palms as I asked:

"You are ill, Miss Austin. May I call your doctor?"

Her hand jerked in my hold. When she answered her voice was stronger:

"I shall be all right now, thank you. Just tired, so very tired. Let me just sit here and rest a while—"

It was true she seemed stronger, but I was not satisfied. Surely this collapse was caused by more than ordinary fatigue. A heart attack—even a light stroke? My life with Aunt Otilda during the last couple of years had made me conscious of the ills of the elderly, and how quickly some weakness might strike. Perhaps delayed shock from Miss Elizabeth's sister's death was responsible. I could not just leave her so.

"Would you like me to call Mrs. Frimsbee—or Irene?"

Her eyes were half-closed and her breath still came in small gasps.

"There is no need to disturb anyone, I assure you." Some of the old firmness had returned to her voice, even though her body still slumped in the chair. "I am much better. I merely was foolish enough to become overtired. Good of you to be concerned, but, yes, I am much better." She spoke as one willing that her words become the truth.

Now she drew her hand out of my grasp, pulled herself up in the rocker. Her expression was one of dismissal. Still, I hesitated to leave her. A soft chime sounded. The hands on the face of the delicate porcelain clock in the center of the mantel pointed to two. What had she been doing up at this hour? She was fully dressed. And, though her bed had been turned down for the night, she had not rested on it.

"Much, much better," she repeated, this time with an emphasis I could not disregard.

"Won't you let me call someone of your family?" I dared to persist, as my conscience (so well trained in Aunt Otilda's school) would not let me just leave her.

"Most kind of you. But I shall do very well now. I am sorry that I disturbed you. I did awaken you, did I not?" Her last question was a bit sharper in tone, her dark eyes probed mine as if my answer was of importance.

"I heard you on the stairs. It was so late, I was afraid something was wrong—" I said. It was not perhaps the truth (for I did not know just what had awakened me), but it was the best I could offer.

"Most kind—" she repeated. Her eyelids drooped.

"Sounds in a house as large and old as this one can be misleading. I hope you have not taken a chill. You had best be back to bed before you do."

The flat dismissal of that I could not disregard. I went out, closing the door behind me. But still I lingered in the chill hall for a moment or two. The faint light below the stairs still shown. Was the light there left on because of what rested in the parlor? I shivered at the thought more than the cold. This house had lost its feeling of stuffy warmth, of overcrowded, antique luxury.

As I slipped along I tried to imagine what could have so shaken my landlady's whalebone-stiffened competence. Also I listened, for what I did not know. But when I gained my own room I tunneled quickly under the bed covers.

It was long before I was able to get back to sleep. So, when I awoke into winter sunlight, my head aching, I saw by my watch that I had overslept.

My throat felt scratchy, an ominous foreshadowing of one of the colds I had come to dread. That warning meant I had better stay in today, in spite of my wish to be elsewhere at the time of the funeral. I checked my bag, laid out cold pills, the inhaler, those preparations winters in this climate had taught me to carry.

What I wanted was a hot breakfast—a leisurely one, where one might linger at the table for a second or even a third cup of coffee and a reading of the morning paper. Yet under the present circumstances I supposed I would have to go out to eat, thus insuring my cold. With sniffling self-pity, I put on my warmest pants suit, and I was just tying a scarf, which was far too cheerful for my morning mood, when there was a perfunctory knock at the door, and the maid who had admitted me four days earlier entered.

"Oh—I am sorry. I thought you had gone out—" She looked startled.

"I overslept. And I think I have caught a cold. I'll go out for breakfast and be back later. I don't want the flu—"

She set down her burden of dustcloths and vacuum.

"You don't have to go out for breakfast, miss, unless you want to. It's laid in the little breakfast room this morning." She skirted the reason for a change in household routine.

Another glance out of the window promised cold and bad walking, while the maid appeared to think that breakfasting here was correct. I went downstairs self-consciously, hoping I would not have to face Miss Elizabeth across what could in no circumstances be termed a festive board.

Only one person was seated at the round table. Preston Donner arose to greet me, one corner of a linen napkin tucked into the opening of his knitted wool waistcoat. He put aside a marmalade-spread square of toast to pull out my chair.

I wished I could think of something bright to add to "Good morning." But any such remarks eluded me.

"You had good weather for your trip with Mrs. Cantrell. Luckily you returned before this closed in." He gestured to the nearest window, which gave a depressing view of bushes hung with accumulations of wet snow. He was taking on the duties of host, pouring me a cup of coffee from a waiting electric pot, pushing a covered bun holder a few inches in my direction. "May I suggest Reena's cinnamon rolls? They are delicious enough to brighten even such a dreary day as this."

Weather—I followed his cue and assured him we had had a pleasant trip, easing thus into a discussion of Theodosia's research. So occupied, I not only made a hearty breakfast, but my feeling of depression lifted. Then Preston Donner, as if he sensed my better mood, changed to a subject nearer home.

"Miss Jansen, I am very glad you decided to come here. Miss Elizabeth gives one the impression that she is armored against all emotional shocks. But that seeming imperviousness is purely a facade. Miss Emma was her sister and, while their lives were in no way similar, and their natures very different, yet there remained a strong family tie. Miss Emma's sudden death—we had all believed that she was recovering very well from her accident—has been a hard blow. Why, Miss Elizabeth and Miss Irene had only visited her only on Sunday and she seemed much better." He made a business of fussily brushing crumbs across the tablecloth. "Now there are few to give Miss Elizabeth any real thought. Miss Irene is very occupied with her husband and her child. Maud and Reena, of course, do all they can to lighten the burden of household care. They have been a part of this house for many years. But neither of them—they are old—can entirely support Miss Elizabeth. Am I—" he asked as he paused and now looked directly at me, "right in believing that you have had experience in dealing with older people?"

"I lived most of my life with an aunt, yes, and of

course, she was of another generation." I was puzzled—did the remaining bits of Aunt Otilda's one-time dominance still *show?*

"Just so. I thought that your attitude when you met Miss Elizabeth for the first time suggested you were not unfamiliar with her—her little eccentricities. Her dress, for example, sometimes astonishes younger women. In this day and age many young people might find her odd. But—more to the point—if Miss Elizabeth should—the number of the family doctor is on a pad by the phone. And my office phone is listed there also. Miss Elizabeth rightly wishes the service this afternoon to be private. But if afterwards she seems to need assistance—" He rolled his napkin to put in a waiting ring.

"I will not be going out today," I answered unhappily. Why had he called upon that morbid feeling of duty to elders, which I had been trying to rid myself of these past months? It was like being jerked back into a box I wanted no more to see. But habit answered for me now: "If Miss Elizabeth needs me, I will be here."

"Thank you!" His voice was too hearty, I decided, as if he had shifted some burden to me. And he went out of the room quickly as if he feared I might recant. But why had he omitted any reference to Sister Anne? Wondering at that, I reached for the paper he had left folded beside his marmalade-smeared plate.

Reena did not cough, shuffle her feet, or display any open impatience, but she made her presence felt, and I knew that I was delaying matters for the kitchen. So I went back upstairs to lay out my notes, though my headache continued in a dull way, and I sniffled. Then

I suddenly struck one of those times so rewarding to a writer, when not only sentences but whole paragraphs flashed into mind. My fingers began to race on the keyboard of my portable, straining to keep up with the spurt of creativity. When my back ached and my neck felt as if it were on fire, I was belatedly aware of time. My watch said half-past twelve—and I remembered now nothing had been said about any lunch.

I sniffed experimentally, decided the nose drops had helped, and got into my coat, inwardly content and still mind-bound on my morning's work. As I went out, Maud came down the hall with a tray. Seeing that brought to my mind Miss Elizabeth's ordeal in the night.

I asked Maud a question.

"No, miss, Miss Elizabeth ain't exactly sick. She's bearing up just wonderful—like she always does when there's trouble. But I'm just taking her a little something to keep up her strength. She has to have that. Miss Anne, she's gone out, and Miss Irene—she eats with the little boy."

"What time is the service?"

"Half-past two, miss. But there ain't going to be many people. Just the family—and Dr. Burton from St. Anthony's to say the words. Miss Emma always said she wanted it that way when she went."

I would have liked to have stayed away from the house until nightfall. But an odd tweak of conscience, triggered by my unwary promise to Preston Donner, made me go straight back after lunch. The old feeling of guilt and worry made me angry with myself—Miss Elizabeth's state of health was no matter to me. I suppose I was still conditioned by Aunt Otilda so that all elderly ladies with that air of command could pull me directly into their service once I came into their orbits.

I was only seven when I had come under Aunt Otilda's domination. Though she had not chosen to wear the dress of the past as Miss Elizabeth did, her mind and emotions were as tightly corseted as Miss Elizabeth's rigid body. So I had been raised by the standards and customs of a period two generations behind my own. Which, of course, had given me an excellent insight to the period I used as a writer, but it had crippled me effectively in my emotional reaction to my own peers. I did not hate Aunt Otilda—at least not consciously. But, though she was dead and I had a feeling of relief which in turn had produced a guilt, I still found it hard to break out of the pattern into which I had been so effectively fitted. So my present uneasy sense of responsibility, Aunt Otilda—Miss Elizabeth—my conditioning still held.

There was a murmur from the parlor as I entered, and the door was half ajar, so that the scent of wilting flowers was doubly strong. I hurried past to the stairs. Still, that sense of duty took me now, not back to my own room and safe removal from the Austin tribe, but down the hall to rap on Miss Elizabeth's door.

At an answering "Come"—I was still farther back in the past.

I opened the door. "It is Erica Jansen, Miss Austin. Is there anything I can do for you?"

Was that moment of silence a rebuke to presumption? I wanted to turn and go. But I was not to escape so easily.

"Do come in."

Miss Elizabeth stood before the old-fashioned bureau. As usual she was dressed in black, this time without any time-yellowed lace. On the tufted spread of the bed rested a toque with pinned-on black veiling, the formal mourning of the generation she had chosen as her own. She did not look around as she spoke.

"Miss Jansen." The tone of her voice cast me back a good fifteen years into my own past. "I have, as you see, completely recovered from my—my fatigue. Completely recovered," she repeated emphatically. "I trust you have not mentioned last night to my sister or my niece?"

So she was afraid of that?

"I have spoken to no one, Miss Austin. Nor shall I—without your wish," I responded.

Her face was reflected in the mirror and there I saw her eyes close for an instant, her mouth tighten. Her shoulders were braced as if she faced some coming trial.

"Most kind," she murmured.

Before I could go, there came a demanding rap on the door and, without waiting for any invitation, Anne Frimsbee entered. Her black crepe dress had been designed to help conceal too plump a hipline, minimize a waist far from willowy. But because of the wearer's poor posture, it did not do its duty. Her blue-tinted hair was arranged to give length to her stocky neck. However, nothing could be done to disguise the wattle of loose flesh under her chin, nor lighten the lines of discontent about her painted mouth.

She frowned at me but, since she remained between

me and the door, I could not yet leave. And it was clear she was very angry.

"Elizabeth!" She made her sister's name a challenge. "The coffin is closed!"

Miss Elizabeth's right hand went to her temple as if to arrange the fringe on her forehead. I had not missed that change in her mirrored eyes, however. To her credit, her voice did not betray her agitation.

"It was Emma's wish that that be done, Anne."

"Nonsense! I know Emma's wishes as well as you do. Nothing could be farther from them. She always wanted to be the center of attention. Well, let her—for the last time! I've made it plain to the men that it is to be opened during the ceremony. The director was most impertinent. I don't see why you selected a man like that to take charge. He actually argued with me! But I made it plain and he understands now. I am going down and make sure that he did do as he was told."

I saw Miss Elizabeth's armor crack. In the few seconds she had listened to that tirade she withered back into the old and helpless woman of the night before. Either Anne Frimsbee did not notice, or she did not care. For she had flounced out of the room.

Miss Elizabeth clung to the edge of the bureau with both hands, staring at her reflection with such stricken eyes that I hurried to her. She was repeating over and over, hardly above a whisper, but in plain panic:

"No, no, no!"

When I would have guided her to a chair, she twisted free of my grasp with a force I did not expect.

"Must—stop—stop—them!" The words came in panting gasps as she lurched towards the door. There was no way I could halt her, I could only go along, give what support she would allow me. She stumbled toward the stairs as if her very life depended upon overtaking Anne.

The murmur of voices below grew louder, as if Anne Frimsbee was still meeting opposition. That sound appeared to goad Miss Elizabeth to a spurt of desperate energy, carrying her down the last few steps and for the moment out of my reach.

"Of course my sister agrees with me! You are to open it—and at once. I never heard such nonsense."

"No!" Miss Elizabeth's protest was a hoarse croak, which apparently did not reach through the now nearly open door.

There were four standing there inside. Anne Frimsbee was directly before the coffin. Her daughter-in-law had retreated a little, as if to get as far from the scene of the dispute as possible. Hanno Horvath scowled at Anne. To him she paid no attention—she was gazing only at the man by the flower-banked coffin.

I caught up with Miss Elizabeth just in time. She had one hand out to the door frame for support, but she swayed. For a moment I thought she was about to faint. But she was still fully conscious—in her face a kind of horror, as if some disaster she had fought valiantly to prevent was now upon her—from which there was no escape.

Though I had no wish to remain, I could not desert Miss Elizabeth in her present state. I tried to catch Hanno Horvath's attention. But he, as well as all the rest, was intent upon Anne and the coffin.

With a small whisper the polished wood and padded silk was raised. Anne Frimsbee, with an expression of complacent triumph, looked down into the interior.

The old legend of Medusa might have been enacted then, for she tensed, and, under her careful makeup, a greenish tinge showed. Her eyes, now wide with shock, were set as if she could not in truth look away.

Miss Elizabeth cried out and slumped, so I had only time to push her into a chair, or her dead weight might have carried me with her to the floor. As I supported her I still watched Anne Frimsbee, wondering if she were about to go into hysterics. The look of her face was like none I had seen before.

There was a sharp exclamation from the man who had opened the coffin. Now Hanno and Irene came closer. Nor could I resist advancing a step or two. Anne's continued horror-stricken paralysis was too compelling.

Exposed to our view were the head and shoulders of a body, but by no means that of an elderly woman.

Rather a youngish man, black hair tousled about his livid face, a look of surprise frozen in eyes and mouth, lay there. And he was wearing the coat of an early nineteenth-century naval uniform, that bright blue coat disfigured on the breast by an irregular brown stain.

"My God!" The words were jolted out of Hanno. He swept a tall basket of white roses out of his path, with force enough to send it spinning across the floor. "How did this happen?" he demanded of the attendant, who in turn was staring at the contents of the coffin in open stupefaction.

"It's Roderick!" Irene's voice scaled up into an eerie shriek.

As if that sound had brought her back to life, Anne Frimsbee whirled. Her hand struck full across her daughter-in-law's face with a sound almost as sharp as a gun-shot, the blow sending Irene back. As the younger woman stumbled and fell, Anne took a single step in her direction, the green, sick look erased from her face by a crimson flood of wild fury as she shouted:

"Shut your damned mouth, you fool!"

Then, as Irene treid to crawl away, tears beginning to stream down her bruised face, Anne clutched at rags of self-control. She glanced around, saw our attention was on her, and faced us, her chin up, and all the arrogance she could assemble coloring her voice.

"That—is—not—my—son—Roderick. Roderick is dead!" She hissed, before she turned and walked out of the room. We stood, like actors frozen in a tableau, until there came the sound of a distantly slammed door.

Miss Elizabeth moaned and I went to her. Since Irene still sat on the floor, rocking back and forth, crying, her hands cupping her face, and since neither of the men had moved, I was impelled to action.

"Please." I glanced first to Hanno, who at least looked as if he had muscles needed in this crisis. "Can you help me get Miss Austin back to her room? I'm afraid she is really ill."

With a muffled ejaculation, he strode over and picked up the old lady, carrying her as if she weighed nothing, taking her upstairs as I hurried along behind. When he laid the now seemingly unconscious woman on her bed, I asked:

"Hadn't the doctor better be called?"

"Yes. I'll do it. Call the police too. Since there has been a murder—apparently—"

I blinked. He had been quick to assess the meaning of that stain on the blue coat. But who—and how—and certainly—why?

Hanno went downstairs, heading, I supposed for the phone. I was left alone to unfold the quilt lying at the foot of the bed over Miss Elizabeth. One question to the fore of my mind—Roderick? Who was Roderick? I searched my memory of Theodosia's outline of the situation, and I did not remember any Roderick—dead or alive—

5

I drew a chair to the side of the bed and sat down. Miss Elizabeth lay crumpled, her breaths coming far too fast, and frightening to hear. How long before the doctor could get here? As for that I had seen downstairs—so I had not been deceived by any bush, shadow, or half-hidden garden statue on the night I had been introduced to the Abbey! I *had* seen that figure in the garden after all. But who—and why? I shook my head as if in so doing I could shake away those questions.

Now I took Miss Elizabeth's restless hands—which were plucking at the cover over her—into mine. Perhaps my steady hold did act as a calming agent. Her head, which had also been turning from side to side as if still to deny all which had just passed, lay quiet now, and her breathing deepened and slowed. I might have thought her asleep, had I not had the disturbing feeling that once or twice I had been spied upon from beneath those heavy eyelids.

"Roderick." I repeated the name to myself. Who *was* Roderick? Mrs. Frimsbee's son—but I had heard him called Charles—

Her violent reaction—certainly that proved she lied in answer to Irene's spontaneous identification. I was sure not even the best of actresses could have counterfeited the extreme shock Anne had registered.

Emma—for the first time I remembered Emma Horvath. With her coffin now tenanted by this strange interloper Roderick, where was Emma? My overstimulated imagination began to play with several grisly possibilities.

Miss Elizabeth must have known something. She had tried hard to prevent this very discovery; again, why? Could she be responsible for the substitution? I found that impossible to believe. I did not think any situation, no matter how desperate, would lead Elizabeth Austin to commit an act so closely approaching desecration. Nor would she have the physical strength to carry it through. Yet the eldest of the Austins had wanted the coffin sealed for burial before the funeral. This must have something to do with the early-morning collapse I had witnessed. Could she have seen the substitution? If so, why had she not protested?

Whatever had happened, I was very sure Miss Elizabeth had acted for what she believed to be the best. She had not kept silent for any personal reason. Therefore—if I were questioned I would choose my answers carefully—

Apart from the desire not to be drawn into a family scandal which was no business of mine, I was determined not to talk. Miss Elizabeth was now, I believed, lying here gathering her forces, trying to rebuild shattered defenses, against a time when she must hold fort to her secrets. I knew myself only too well the pain of broken reserves, how one writhed when there were breaches through which one's inner emotions might be betrayed. No, I would volunteer nothing. Any questions I would answer as tersely as possible.

I wished I dared offer Miss Elizabeth that reassurance, but I thought that to speak now, to force her out of her hiding, would undo all the good of these moments of rest she was being allowed. Then my dilemma was solved by Maud and the doctor entering together. As she passed me, the maid said in a low voice:

"The police are downstairs, miss. They want to talk to everyone, they said."

I had the usual private citizen's reaction to that news the law wanted to talk to me: a feeling of sudden nervous guilt even when my conscience was clear—and at this moment that was slightly clouded. I was somehow convinced they might see straight through any evasions I might try.

"Severe shock is never good at her age." The doctor addressed me as if I were in charge. "I shall give her a sedative and then make sure they don't try to question her—not today anyway."

"A nice cup of tea. Miss Elizabeth likes a nice cup of tea when she is upset-like. Herb tea, it is. Miss Elizabeth gets it special—she says it's better than medicine." Maud broke in.

The doctor nodded. "Yes, try that. And later perhaps some of Reena's soup. Then, if she rouses in the night, one of these pills. But don't talk to her. Discourage it if she tries to discuss what has happened. We don't want her dwelling on that."

That, I was sure, was the last thing Miss Elizabeth would want to do. I would wager that she was not any longer as exhausted as she seemed, and that the mind behind the netted hair and forehead fringe was already at work, trying to find a solution to some problem I could not begin to understand. Perhaps the doctor knew this patient well enough to deduce that also. For he reiterated that Miss Elizabeth was not to be left alone, not to miss taking the pill. As he was about to leave, the door was flung open with force. Anne Frimsbee stood on the threshhold.

How long had it been since that scene in the parlor—an hour? It seemed more. But in that time she had aged nearly a generation. Yet in spite of that surface crumbling, she blazed with determination as her eyes swept from the doctor to the quiet figure on the bed. She attempted to come closer, but the doctor quickly thwarted her.

"Let me see Liz!"

"Not now, Anne, and I mean that!" There was iron in his voice. "She must not be disturbed. That shock was very bad for her."

"The shock?" Her tone dismissed that as nonsense. "Liz must listen to reason. Do you know what they're saying now, do you, John Bains? They're saying that—that body is *Roderick!* He's dead—you know it—all of us know it. He died in that car crash in Italy two years ago. Just because he made some mistakes and people hounded him, he had to go abroad. And he died and was buried. You saw the telegram yourself, don't deny it. I want Liz to help me make those—those police understand it's all a vicious lie! That fool Irene yelling it out like that—when she knows it wasn't the truth. Liz—" She raised her voice. "You get up and come down. Maybe they'll listen to you and stop believing lies—"

The doctor's hand was on Anne's arm, and I saw him give her a shake.

"Be quiet! She can't hear you—I've given her a sedative. She is asleep and will be for hours. Under no circumstances is she to be disturbed. Understand that, Anne? I will tell the police the same thing."

"The police!" Her face flushed almost purple. "I'd like to know who called them." Her outstretched fingers curled into claws. "I'd like to get my hands on whoever did it. I tell you one thing, I'm not going to listen to any more lies!" She turned and rushed away and I heard a door down the hall slam.

The doctor shook his head. "It *is* Roderick, of course," he said almost to himself. "And good riddance. If only he had not turned up here as he did. One thing is true—Miss Emma and some friends managed to cover up for that young thug before. It can't be done this time. I'm only sorry for Miss Elizabeth. She must not be disturbed." Now he spoke directly to me, and for the first time it seemed to register with him that I was a stranger. Quickly I explained my position in the house and added I would do anything I could. To my rather shamed relief he shook his head now.

"As a comparative stranger, Miss Jansen, she might find you disturbing, I will suggest that Maud, with Reena's help of course, take care of her."

Maud smoothed down her apron. "Yes sir, that we will!" There was pride in her voice. "Miss Elizabeth ain't going to see nobody unless you say she do, Dr. Bains, I promise that!"

So I could not seek any refuge in the sickroom. On the other hand I was not going to voluntarily insert my head into the lion's jaws. I was on my way back to my own room, when Leslie Lowndes came quickly up the stairs, a mink coat flung back on her shoulders. Her blond hair was uncovered and she was breathing hard.

"Miss Jansen, can you give me a sensible answer as to what in the world is going on? They called me back from the office, and now some police sergeant tells me to stay until I am asked questions. As if I am going to sit down there waiting for what I don't know! What *has* happened?"

I outlined the events of the immediate past and her annoyance vanished, in complete surprise.

"But what a bizarre—unbelievable thing! Roderick Frimsbee—after all these years! Oh, yes, I heard of the family black sheep. He was caught drug-running or something a few years back—but the family had disowned him before that. Miss Emma used to speak her mind about his horrid reputation and how hard it was for dear innocent Charles to live it down, being in the service and all. But he was dead—at least that's what they said—killed abroad in a car accident. And if he's in the coffin now—*where* is Miss Emma?"

"I imagine that is what the police are trying to find

out—or one of the things. Roderick was apparently shot—"

"Shot!" she echoed and shook her head. "But things like that simply do *not* happen to the Austins—"

A thick-set man of middle age appeared at the foot of the stairs to look up at us both. He carried the authority of the law in every plane of his heavy, jowled face.

"Now, Miss Lowndes." He addressed Leslie. "Weren't you told to sit and wait in that room?"

"I was ordered around in my own home without any explanation." She flared. "You'd get a lot farther with reasonable people if you showed a fraction of common sense, Sergeant or Inspector or whatever you claim to be. I'm neither a moron nor a child."

"In the room downstairs—*if* you please." He looked as if he meant to escort her every step of the way and then take other measures to insure she stayed there.

"You, too, miss." He consulted a notebook. "You are Mrs. Irene Frimsbee?"

"No." Perhaps my denial was too vehement. But I had had enough of the Frimsbees and the Austins. "I am Erica Jansen."

"Yes." He consulted the notebook again and nodded. "Well, the lieutenant wants to see you, too. Downstairs, if you please."

Leslie went without any other further protest and I followed. We were herded into the breakfast room, and had no chance to exchange comments on the weird happening of the afternoon, as a young patrolman took a seat by the door and so remained an ever-present warning.

Leslie threw her mink into another chair, lit a cigarette, and went to stand by the window, staring out into the black and white of the neglected garden. I was hungry, the after-effect for me of any emotional upset. So my speculations hovered around as to when we would be released and perhaps allowed to leave the house in search of food. All my contact with police procedures came mainly from fiction. I am devoted to crime novels —mainly of the old-fashioned house-party-butler-in-the-pantry-all-right-with-the-village-gossips   school. Which was not much use to me in judging what was going to happen next.

Were we all under suspicion of shooting, or perhaps using a knife, to bring that black sheep of the Austin clan his present resting place? Had any woman strength enough to effect the exchange of bodies by herself? What *had* Miss Elizabeth taken part in, or witnessed at two in the morning?

I did not want to think about that, and I hoped I would not inadvertently betray it in my questioning. It was Miss Elizabeth's own business, and none of mine. The dragging minutes crawled by, and I felt we had been there for hours. Then the stolid man stood once more in the doorway.

"Miss Jansen, please." He summoned me.

Leslie glanced at me, her annoyance plain. I was divided between the relief of my wait being over, and my apprehension. Thus I found myself for the first time in the library of the house, a solemn room paneled in the darkest of oak, one huge, stained-glass window behind the mammoth desk—giving the impression of a church

and altar. From behind the desk, a man arose to introduce himself as Lieutenant Daniels.

He was polite and mannered, and because of that,
even more intimidating. I sat down in the chair he indicated, and answered the routine questions of name,
permanent address, and the reason for my being here.
A young man, half in the shadows, took it all down in
shorthand.

"Then you have only been here since Sunday, Miss
Jansen?"

"Really less than that." I told of my trip with Theodosia.

"You moved in Sunday morning, you left before
noon with Mrs. Cantrell, you returned with her yesterday. Had you any acquaintance with the Austins prior
to your arrival here?"

"No, I met Miss Elizabeth Austin for the first time
Saturday night—also Mrs. Irene Frimsbee. Her mother-
in-law later."

"I see." Lieutenant Daniels leaned forward. His
voice was friendly, encouraging. "Was there anything
which happened Saturday night which was out of the
ordinary?"

I wavered. Should I tell him of what I had seen in
the garden? I had not mentioned it to anyone. To do
so now might put me into the category, as far as the
lieutenant was concerned, of a seeker of notoriety, eager to make myself important. Yet—to keep quiet—I
could not decide. But some change of expression must
have given me away.

"There was something—what?"

No use to try and conceal it now. Even my momentary dithering might have already raised some suspicion. I told my tale as badly as I could—hoping he would not believe it was a flight of afterthought imagination.

"You did not mention this to Mr. Donner, nor to Miss Austin. Why?"

"Because it was too fantastic. There are statues in the garden—it was night and the wind blew the shrubs around. I could have seen something and just thought it was a naval officer of the 1800s. Who would believe a real one was lurking in the garden?"

"Mrs. Cantrell had served cocktails—"

At that remark I came close to losing my temper. The implication made me bristle. Borrowing that frigid tone Aunt Otilda had cultivated for her own use, I answered frostily:

"I accepted one small glass of sherry, of which I had about two sips. It happens I dislike the taste of most drinks and do not take them."

He eyed me as if he would like to get inside my head and sort out my thoughts and memories to his own advantage.

"Who suggested that you visit Miss Austin right then? Did you or Mr. Donner insist upon it?"

"He did. I think he was eager for Miss Austin to rent the room I now have. I have been told that the upkeep of this house is a worry to her, and she depends very much on her paying guests."

"And you never met this helpful Mr. Donner before, either?"

"No. The only person I knew before Saturday night was Mrs. Cantrell. I was introduced to her through my publisher some time ago. We met by chance at the library here, where we are both doing research. She invited me for Saturday night." I made it simple and terse, but I was thinking fast. I could see his side of it—why had I been so quick to follow Preston Donner's suggestion? I remembered my uneasiness at the time—and now I could not really understand how I had been so swept along.

"Now give me your version of what happened here this afternoon." He changed the subject.

I swallowed a sigh of relief. At least he no longer picked at motives which, I had to admit myself, looked and sounded odd. Again I confined myself to what I hoped was a reasonably accurate account of the fantastic scene—beginning with that moment when Mrs. Anne Frimsbee had come into Miss Elizabeth's room and proceeding to the time when Hanno Horvath had carried Miss Austin back to her chamber. I omitted my own suspicion that Miss Elizabeth had known what was going to be disclosed when the coffin was opened. After all, that was only conjecture on my part.

"I then stayed with Miss Austin until the doctor arrived. When I left her room, I was told to wait down here."

"Interesting" was his comment. Then he dismissed me and I went back to my own room.

I was hungry. Unfortunately my metabolism is such that if I did not heed the warning of hunger, I would end with a bad headache. Dare I, under the circumstances, invade the kitchen and ask Reena for a snack? As propriety and hunger struggled, I watched through my window the coming and going of the police. A knot of spectators, in spite of the nasty weather, had gathered by the gate, watching the house as if they expected flames to come shooting from the roof.

Even if we were free to go, I did not want to face that crowd. Then I considered going to Theodosia. Did she even know what had happened?

Maud—perhaps it would be better to brave Maud instead of Reena. If Miss Elizabeth was asleep, maybe Maud would be willing to let me know the possibility of food. As I went into the hall, I ran into Leslie the second time.

Her face was tired, shadowed. For once she looked vulnerable. She gave me an uncertain smile and became a warmer and more friendly person.

"I'm completely done in," she reported. "And I think they are not going to let us out of the madhouse for dinner."

"I don't think you'd want to go. There's a crowd at the street gate."

"Oh, lord. No doubt complete with reporters." Leslie's shoulders sagged a fraction. "The press—what a field day they'll have with this! It's a story with everything as far as they are concerned. All right, so we're in a stage of siege. Are you game to tackle Reena and see what we can do?"

"I thought of asking Maud."

"And a bright thought that is. Reena can be a handful. Where is Maud, in with Miss Elizabeth? By the way, how is Miss Elizabeth?"

"The doctor gave her a sedative. The shock was bad for her."

"I can imagine! After all, it must have been one for everybody—"

"Except," I commented, "the one responsible."

Leslie opened her door and tossed her coat on the bed.

"Yes. It looks as if someone was very desperate for a cover-up—or else has a devilish sense of humor—or both." She went to the mirror above the dressing table. As she spoke, she leaned forward to study her reflection, not in admiration, but critically, as she might study some tool she had a use for. But she did not reach for any of the boxes and jars in wide array at hand. Rather, she turned away again.

"Let's see Maud and then tackle Reena if we have to. I take it Anne and Irene haven't appeared yet?"

I had no intention of describing the scene in the parlor between Anne Frimsbee and her daughter-in-law. "No."

"They have Preston in for questioning, and Hanno's waiting. That makes four of us, at least. Well—on to the kitchen!"

I was perfectly willing to allow her the initiative, and so listened as she talked to a very unhelpful Maud through a crack of opening at Miss Elizabeth's door.

"That's that," she said at last. "Maud is sticking by her post. We'll have to face Reena on our own. We'd better do it now."

The back stairs were dark and only one-half the width of the front, ending in an entryway. Leslie pushed through a swinging door and we were in a large kitchen. Though the big range of an earlier day had been banished for a modern stove, and a large refrigerator and a dishwasher stood against the wall, the room still had a Victorian look.

By a bow window was a cushioned rocker, flanked by a small table. In this chair Reena sat, her impassive face stubbornly turned toward the paved courtyard outside, toward the old stable now converted to a garage. I must admit that had I faced the cook alone, I would have retreated in confusion. Not so Leslie. Whatever demands her job might make, a gift of handling the stubborn must have been part of her training—though at first Reena replied only in grunts, while Leslie took it upon herself to explore cupboards and store shelves. The cook at last heaved her bulk out of the rocker and padded across the floor.

Having stirred Reena to labor, Leslie was wise enough to take the rank of assistant. I hung my jacket on the back of the rocker and cleaned up after them. The savory smells proceeding from Reena's efforts were payment enough for our efforts. Maud came down to fix a tray for Miss Elizabeth, and she agreed to ask Irene if she wanted a tray for Stuart.

I went back and forth, setting the table in the breakfast room. There were still sounds from the front of the house—masculine voices. Once a door slammed. But no one came to the back quarters. So I was startled by the appearance of Preston Donner, who put out a hand to halt me.

"How is Miss Elizabeth?"

I repeated my report of the doctor and of Maud's attendance.

"Good, good!" He turned to look out of the window,

and I guessed he was sorting his own thoughts, not really interested in any view of the dreary dusk.

Leslie volunteered to summon the Frimsbees. I was not surprised when she reported they refused to come down. The food was good, and I was hungry. Leslie matched me bite for bite. Hanno Horvath chewed each mouthful with machinelike thoroughness. Preston Donner drank coffee, played with a couple of spoonfuls of stew he had transferred to his plate. But I thought he actually ate nothing much.

When we took our plates back to the kitchen we found Irene Frimsbee there, pouring milk into a mug. She averted her face as if caught in some embarrassing act, snatched up a tray, and started for the back stairs. If Leslie noticed the darkening bruise on Irene's cheek, she made no comment.

Once we had tidied up, Leslie seemed to lose all desire for company. She left abruptly, and must have shut herself at once in her room as I did not see her again. Back in my chamber I kicked off my shoes, but did not undress. Settling down in the wing chair near the window, I closed my eyes. I must have slept.

Light flashing in my eyes awakened me. I looked out to see a car coming up the drive. The police again? How long would they stay—and would we have another round of questions?

Pure curiosity, and nothing else, took me out in the hall. That was as dark as it had been the night before. My slippered feet made no sound as I padded along to the head of the stairs. I had even gone down two steps, though I was still, luckily, out of sight from below, when I froze.

Were my ears playing tricks? Or was this really a part of a singularly realistic dream? I refused to believe that I had correctly identified that voice. With only the instinct for flight left in me, I spun around and headed for my room.

But I never reached the refuge. For down at the other end of the hall, a shadow seemed to detach itself from the wall. It floated without any sound towards the back stairs.

6

That shadowy figure had almost reached the head of the back staircase when there sounded the distant ringing of the phone. With a muffled cry, the half-seen figure clutched at the wall. I heard a bumping sound as if some object had fallen and was rolling from step to step.

The phone ceased—it might have been answered. In the quiet the shadow disappeared down the staircase. I followed, keeping far enough behind, I hoped, not to be seen. Though the stairs were dark, a panel of light shone out of the kitchen into the side entry below. Either Reena had not yet retired, or someone else was there.

Clinging to the rail with one hand, as she stooped to retrieve a flashlight lying on the floor, was Miss Elizabeth. On her head was the veiled toque she had prepared for the funeral, and an old sealskin coat covered her from throat to ankle. She must be planning to go out.

I wondered where Maud could be, as Miss Austin paused before the kitchen door to look in. Her halt there, I was sure, would be brief. I stumbled back up the hall to pull on shoes in frantic haste, dive into my coat. I was still struggling to get an arm into that as I ran back.

Miss Elizabeth was no longer in sight. Out which door? I did not know my way around the kitchen quarters very well. Trying to keep my own descent as noiseless as possible, I hurried down.

Reena's chair was vacant. The chain was up in place at the back door. So my quarry had not left that way. The side door then—

I tiptoed down the hall, not wanting to attract any attention from those in the front of the house. The sound of that one voice had shaken me badly. Though how and why *he* had come here—the sensible thing to do would be to arouse help, but somehow I still could not betray Miss Elizabeth, even though it might be for her own good.

Physically, I was sure, she had been incapable of accomplishing the exchange of bodies. But I no longer doubted she had known something about it, and, for her own reasons, had been willing to keep the substitution a secret—willing to allow her nephew to be buried in her sister's place.

There came a faint click, which could have been that of a door lock eased into place. I must hurry if I was not to lose Miss Elizabeth in the wilds of the garden.

The night air was crisp as I edged out through the side door, cold enough to make me wish I had brought a scarf for my head, while a few steps only made plain my folly of tramping here without boots.

A flicker of light drew me on, past a growth of bush which was a screen for the lower story of the house. Here was a walk which must run parallel with that connecting the Horvath property to the Abbey. I glanced back. Except for the partially blocked glow of the kitchen light, the Abbey was dark on this side.

Miss Elizabeth must believe she was free of fear of observation, for her flashlight was on and held steady—its light catching now and then the edge of the veil blowing about her tall figure.

I dropped back. Though she had not looked behind as yet, she might at any moment. The path made an abrupt turn—now I could see a light from the carriage house. If the inhabitants of the Abbey were mostly safely in bed, the Cantrells were keeping much later hours. For a moment I was tempted to go after Theodosia. If I had known Miss Austin's goal I would have done just that.

A figure came into view on the carriage path, and for a hopeful instant I thought it might be Theodosia. Though why she might be roaming the Abbey garden at this hour—then the other was silhouetted against the distant light and showed itself to be unmistakably masculine.

I had no wish to meet this new lurker in the garden. Two steps took me into cover among the clutches of bushes. But I discovered that, behind that screen, I could still follow the guide of Miss Elizabeth's flashlight.

The chill of the ground struck up into my feet. It seemed even worse when I scrambled back on the walk again. Icy fingers of wind thrust down into my coat collar. Miss Elizabeth's flashlight suddenly winked out. I was afraid now, even willing for her to learn I had followed her for the sake of her company. Anything was better than being alone in this dark.

The walk made another abrupt turn, so I was able to avoid by only an inch or so a painful encounter with a wrought-iron bench. Through the bare branches of trees I now caught the beam of a street light.

However, the walk did not end at the bench. There the snow-covered pavement split, one segment curving towards the Horvath estate, the other angling right. The tracks in the half-frozen slush led in the latter direction.

Next came a wall of dense shrubbery, towering higher than my head. There the walk did end, in a small paved area, before an iron gate hung from posts set in the brush. Beyond, the circle of the flashlight jerked from side to side, as if Miss Elizabeth was seeking something on the ground. I tried the gate, it swung open easily without a sound.

Her flashlight swept across a pallid object, which I identified with a shiver. There was no mistaking the purpose of that upright slab of stone. Miss Elizabeth had come to a private graveyard. Now the circle of light flashed up, centered on something Miss Austin held in her other hand.

Though the wind sighed I was able to catch a few of

the words she read—their solemn cadence added to my uneasiness. The light wavered once more to the ground, skirting a mound covered by a tarpaulin, as Miss Elizabeth knelt. Her hand came into the path of the light, picked up a clod of earth and let it fall with sullen finality into the dark hole. Borne by some trick of the wind, her voice was unusually distinct and clear.

"—we commend the soul of our dear sister departed, and we commit her body to the ground—"

Miss Elizabeth was reading the burial service above an empty grave prepared for that afternoon's funeral, which had been so strangely interrupted. She—had she lost her mind?

I edged back until the iron gate pressed against my shoulders. Help—I must get help! Either from the Cantrells' or the Abbey. With a shaking hand I opened the gate, clinging to its solid support, my head still turned to watch the figure by the grave. What would Miss Elizabeth do—return to the house now? What might happen if she discovered she was being watched?

Thoroughly shaken, I stepped free of the gate and started back along the walk. The Cantrells—those at the Abbey—the police—which? If I went to the Abbey the police would be drawn in. I reached the parting of the paths again, still unable to make up my mind.

The scrape of a foot on the walk startled me. Miss Elizabeth! I wheeled about. Only moments before I had thought of her with sympathy. Now I shrank from meeting her face to face.

I grasped the snow-wet back of the bench, sure that in this dark, if I did not move, I might escape notice.

But a moment later there came a shrill cry, a scream so eerie that it almost tore an answering shriek from me.

I heard the grate of metal on stone, the thud of running feet. Shrinking back into the bushes, I watched a dark figure totter by. That must have been Miss Elizabeth, frightened away from her labor of conscience. By what or whom?

At that moment I decided I had had enough, of the Abbey, of all connected with it. As soon as my feet would obey me again I would go to Theodosia. If the Cantrells would not or could not shelter me for the night, they would at least have the charity to let me call a taxi and so reach the inn.

As yet my escape was not possible. I was afraid to venture out of hiding. There remained who or what had so startled Miss Austin into her screaming flight. Or had it been that her nerves had given away? I bit hard on my underlip, my nails dug into my sweating palms. I tried counting slowly. When I reached a hundred I would move—down to the carriage house.

Then my common sense returned. I could move—it was only a matter of putting one foot before the other. Also, I could hear nothing now but the wind.

Still straining my ears, I crawled from behind the bench. Then the very ordinary sound of a car being driven along the street outside the wall brought matters into reasonable focus. "Ghosts, goblins, things that go bump in the night!" I scorned my panic.

Head up, ashamed of my silly fright, I started on between the overhanging bushes, the path so dark in some places that I had to stretch my hands before me to feel an open way. My imagination was busy. Why, at this particular moment, did my thoughts prod me with a nasty tale by M. R. James, in which a black and tattered Thing scuttled through brush, dogging the path of any who walked in a cursed wood after nightfall?

There was an excellent answer to the Thing—a beam from a street light. As wild and lonesome as the garden might appear, it was, I must remember, in a very ordinary and modern small city. Just a few yards away was a bus stop. Beyond that lights controlled traffic—cars passed—

My hand flew to my mouth. I wavered back into the thorn-studded arms of a shrub, to recoil again, branches tearing at my hair and coat. One whipped my cheek, scoring the skin. But I concentrated on those sounds—footsteps—muffled, but still regular—and behind me. I was being followed!

Finding the path again I plunged forward so violently I slipped and came near to losing my balance. A moment later I was down on my hands and knees. Paying no attention to scraped palms and torn hose, I somehow fought my way up, miserably certain my floudering had betrayed me to my pursuer.

The street lamp I had counted on as a guide was now blotted out. It was not until I crashed against a closed door that I realized I had reached another building. Beneath my frantic fingers, the knob that my groping discovered refused to turn. I was locked out of what might be a refuge.

With one hand on the wall for a guide, I edged along, hoping to put this place, whatever it might be, between me and my follower. I longed to pause, to listen, but I dared not.

The building seemed large. It was a long time before I reached the corner of the wall. Here the ground gave way beneath my feet, and I fell again, so suddenly that a cry was jarred out of me.

My cry was answered by a call I was too confused and frightened to answer. On hands and knees I crawled on. Under me was a cold sweep of concrete—a driveway? But that meant a gate—a way to the street and safety! But I was so confused that somehow I found my way not out—but back once more to the building.

There was shouting—as if more than one person was chasing me. Or was that rather the sounds of help on its way from the Abbey? I cowered against the wall, panting, my hands scraped raw, pressed to my face. Could I escape the attention of any pursuer until that help arrived?

Then a beam of light pinned me there, blinded me. I heard a sharp exclamation of surprise.

"A woman!"

I think I was a little hysterical by that time. What had he expected—Dracula? My panic was ebbing. Surely no assailant would use a light, not with others near by. There *were* others, I could hear their noisy progress through the garden.

"Who is it?" came a call from not too far away.

"A woman—" repeated my captor.

Only two short words, but at their repetition I drew a sharp breath which was both dissent and protest. Even five years—it was not fair, I told myself, to have this in addition to what I had just gone through.

Once more I was gripped by the desire to laugh. Of

all the possible meetings with Mark Rohmer which my imagination had presented from time to time, one such as this had never occurred to me. I was conscious of my bedraggled condition. What a pity that fainting at such crucial and embarrassing moments was now out of fashion. How easily ladies had been able to escape from such awkward confrontations in the days when one could, no, was even expected to, swoon. The situation which had frightened me like a nightmare was about to end in a shaming farce.

Well, I would have to face this. I had made a long run, far longer than just across the end of the Abbey garden, to avoid this moment. Now I was heartened by discovering in myself an unexpected source of strength to stiffen my backbone and produce a voice sounding reassuringly cool. If he had not suspected my identity, it might be my turn to provide a shock—unless I had been totally dismissed from his mind long ago.

"I would appreciate not being blinded, please."

When he did not answer, or switch away the light, I was provoked and somewhat angry. Could it be true he had no memory of me at all? Somehow I found that irritating rather than reassuring.

"Are you a policeman?".

He could not be. What *was* Mark Rohmer doing here?

"If one cannot cross the garden without being chased and frightened—" I continued, my confidence returning with every word.

This was wonderful! Why, I need never have feared such confrontation at all! Seeing Mark had not reduced me to the depths of shame. I must only hold on to this new sense of power, of self-confidence. After all this time, I was truly cured!

The light dropped at last. I lowered my hands from my face where I had used them to shade my eyes. Then the others were upon us from out of the garden and I heard Preston Donner say, in astonishment and concern:

"Why—it's Miss Jansen!"

If he had not recognized me before—at least Mark must now. As for me, I wanted to get away while I was still buoyed up with this unusual sense of detachment.

"I would like to return to the house, Mr. Donner, if you are all through playing hide and seek," I announced. "I think I have been sufficiently frightened for one evening." I held out one hand in the direction of Donner's voice, ignoring the still-unseen Mark.

"Of course." He came swiftly into the beam of light and I clutched his arm with more fervor than I had ever before accepted any masculine support. My legs were shaking. Perhaps I was not so armored as I had believed a moment ago. Or perhaps my exertions of the past half-hour were responsible for this queer, weak feeling. I did want to get away from Mark as soon as possible.

"If you don't mind, Mr. Donner, I would like to get in. I became lost in the garden, and then I was chased by the man holding that light." I made my words sound as stiff a protest as I could.

Donner's support was firm and ready. It gave me the secure feeling I needed. Still, Mark said nothing at all as I was towed gently away. Donner snapped on his own flashlight to show our path. I went eagerly, still

tense, still expecting to hear even a single word of protest. When that did not come, I was perversely angry.

Now I was fully aware of my smarting hands, my
soaked feet and hair. I must look like a perfect witch.
No wonder he had not known me. I was grateful for
Preston Donner, the ever-perfect gentleman of a model
I had sometimes been—reluctantly—exposed to in
Aunt Otilda's narrow world.

"I was only going over to see Mrs. Cantrell." My
voice sounded peevish, and I did not try to correct
that. "And I became mixed up on the paths in the
dark. Then that very officious policeman started chasing me. And, well, I didn't know he was the police—"
Babbling, yes, but that explanation was the first which
came into my mind at the moment. I was not going to
say more until I had time to do some uninterrupted
thinking.

There was warm pressure on my arm, a note of
comfort in his voice as he answered:

"A most frightening experience. I trust you are not
hurt?"

"Just a few minor scrapes and bumps." I was very
glad to see the side door not too far ahead.

However, when once within the house again, I had
some difficulty in persuading my too-sensitive cavalier
that I could indeed proceed by myself, achieving my
way only after some argument. Miss Elizabeth's door
was firmly closed as I went down the upper hall. I
paused by it. Under my touch the knob turned, I must
satisfy myself—I looked in.

From the bureau top, a shaded lamp gave very limited light. Miss Elizabeth lay in the bed, two braids of

hair, as white as the linen of the pillow cases, resting over her shoulders to prove she had retired for the night. On the chaise longue Maud rested, her prim cap askew, her black and gray hair straggling from its daytime knot. Her breath bubbled between her lips in a series of snorts. But someone had pulled the folds of an afghan over her body.

Save for that, I could not criticize the innocent-appearing stage setting. Whoever might come to investigate—if that did happen—would see no more than was proper for that hour. I guessed that if I attempted to arouse the mistress of the house, I would be treated to an excellent performance of a dazed old lady being shaken from a much-needed rest. Not that I was going to put Miss Elizabeth to any such test. Even the door was unlocked, though I was certain Miss Austin did not so usually invite any invasion of her privacy. This scene had been arranged to entice a viewing of innocence at rest.

Once more I wanted to laugh. But I closed the door as quietly as I had opened it and went on to my own room.

There I took inventory of my deplorable condition. My shoes—I kicked off those swishy blobs—could probably never be worn again. My pantyhose were a mass of runs, spreading up and down from bloody knees. There were splatters of melting snow on my coat, circles of damp on my slacks. My hair hung in sodden rings across my face.

Late as it was, I had to trust in soundproofed walls and soak in a tub. I was shivering, and my cold was certainly going to be much worse unless I applied some heroic measures.

Wrapped in my robe, I went down the hall and soaked. Then, feeling really warm again, I turned to the serious task of dealing with my hair. I was twirling rollers with veteran ease, when there came a knock at my door. I froze—but of course it could *not* be—

"Who's there?"

"Leslie." There was, I thought, a demanding inflection in that indentification.

"Come in." I must stick to that story I had told Donner—he had seemed to accept it without question. The trouble was I thought Leslie Lowndes might be a little less ready to believe in such foolish action on anyone's part.

She might have been just aroused from a well-earned rest, but her blue caftan was fashion-inspired, and she apparently did not sleep in either face cream or rollers. Or else she had waited to get rid of them before venturing out of sanctuary.

"What's going on? Someone in the bathroom at this hour—lights all over the garden. This is the middle of the night! What do the police think they are doing?"

"It is really very simple." I must not let her seem formidable. Was my present confidence born of the fact that the worst I had expected had now happened and the world had not come to an end—rather, I was in firm command of myself? I was not even too conscious of the rollers, of my semi-broiled face. "I was going over to see Theodosia, and one of the police must have followed me. I took a wrong turn and got lost. Then he started chasing me and scared me out of my wits. I had no idea who he was—"

I watched Leslie's reflection in the mirror behind my own. Had or had not her head moved a fraction at my mention of the garden? That man on the path earlier—someone coming to the house? But I was certain Leslie was not going to challenge my story. And I had the rest of the night to polish it—iron out any weaknesses.

My exultation grew. This feeling of being in command of my destiny—it was wonderful! I watched my lips curve into a small smile. Despite rollers and no powder on my shiny nose, I had, I thought critically, never looked better in my life. Then, remembering my audience, I yawned.

"I'm guilty about the bathroom. Sorry I disturbed you, but I came in soaked and took a precaution against a chill."

"I understand." Leslie moved back to the door. "It must have been a most frightening experience."

She was interrupted by a rap. I stiffened and then forced myself to relax, dared to ask a favor. Waving an explanatory hand towards the door, and then to my head, I whispered:

"Will you see who that is?"

She nodded, opening the door a thin crack to ask: "Who is it?"

"Miss Jansen?" inquired a masculine voice, kept to a corresponding whisper. It was not the one I had feared to hear.

Leslie glanced at me. I had already kicked off my

slippers and was shedding my robe. Then I spoke, loud enough to be heard outside.

"I have had a very disturbing time and I am going to bed. Since I do not want to catch the flu I shall remain there."

Leslie smiled and nodded. Then she slipped out to confront my midnight caller, apparently to testify I was doing exactly what I had said. I waited but heard nothing more. Then I turned out the light, and, for the first time in my life, locked my bedroom door before going to bed.

7

In spite of my desire for thinking out what had happened in the garden, I fell into the deepest sleep I had known for days shortly after I stretched out between those chilly sheets. When I roused, I was half within another dream, one I tried to prolong but which, after the manner of our best dreams, swiftly faded.

As I sat up in bed I saw the draggled clothing I had dropped the night before. Certainly I was right in thinking I would never be able to wear those shoes again. The suit must be sent to the cleaners. I would have to wear my best, whether I wanted to or not. Having been raised to believe that the wearing of "best" was done only on important occasions, I began some planning to justify it.

The feeling of freedom which had carried over from my dream puzzled me. This energy, the desire to be doing—doing what I did not exactly know—was new. My thoughts kept turning to those moments when I had met Mark face to face and stood my ground. He never, I told myself exultantly, could guess I carried a burden from the past—that was pure sentimental trash, nonsense!

I needed only to continue as I had last night, and I would have no worries. Did Leslie, and those poised women like her, always feel this sort of self-confidence?

Shedding my rollers, I regarded the result in the mirror. Under a scarf, it should not look too bad. I knew I was going to get out of the Abbey. I wanted to see Theodosia, buy a new pair of shoes—take a shopping tour.

Now I transferred my wealth of possessions from the plain plastic handbag which did daily duty to the elegant snakeskin box which matched my best pumps. Nine-thirty by my watch. There was a car parked in the drive, another closer to the gate. Perhaps I had better take the garden path to the coach house.

I paused in the hall. One more duty. I tapped on Miss Austin's door. It opened just enough for Maud to squeeze through. Her face was not quite as dourly set as usual, as she looked at me.

"How is Miss Austin?"

"Sleeping, miss. Ever since last night. And she's going to keep on sleeping as far as them police know. She's been all shook up, Miss Elizabeth has, and that ain't good—not at her age."

"She won't be disturbed with you on guard, Maud."

" 'Deed she won't, miss! I've been with her all night, and the poor dear lady slept like a lamb. Nobody's going to get in to trouble her, not while I'm around. You going out, miss?"

"Yes. Anything I can get for Miss Austin?"

"No, miss. Not that I know of. But thank you kindly, just the same." She retreated crabwise into the room and closed the door. I almost lingered to listen for the sound of a barricade in erection. It would be a very determined law-enforcement officer who would dare to enter that fortress.

I went to the lower hall and looked up Theodosia's phone number. A distant ringing made me impatient. I wanted to get out of the house.

"Theodosia?"

"Just a minute." Gordon, and by his tone in no good mood. But Theodosia's warmth of greeting a moment later made up for his curtness.

"Erica, what in the world is going on? I have called five times, got some policeman, but no logical answer. And somebody came over last night with the weirdest list of questions. He froze me out when I tried to ask some of my own. Has there been more trouble? And what's going on down by the old theater?"

As she paused for breath I managed a question: "What theater?"

"The little one—where the Austins used to give the Jane Austen plays—I told you. There are two police cars and an ambulance there, and they won't let anyone near. Ordered Gordon away when he tried to go over this morning. What *has* happened?"

I was not prepared to tell the story over the phone. Perhaps if I did not bolt for freedom now I might be stopped by Lieutenant Daniels or one of his zealous underlings.

"Listen, Theodosia, I have to go downtown. Are you going to the library this morning? Can I get a ride?"

"Do they have you in a state of siege? No, I'm not going in, but Gordon is, and he'll give you a lift. Come over, I'll even provide breakfast if you haven't eaten. But you'll have to tell all in return."

"I'll be there." But as I put down the phone, I wondered if I would be able to escape.

Irene Frimsbee came down the stairs. I could hear the distant crying of a fretful child. Her face, bruised as it was, also showed drawn and haggard, her eyes tired. Over her arm was the plaid coat, and she had a scarf tied over her head.

"Are you going out, Mrs. Frimsbee?"

She stared at me glassily, looking, I thought, as if she had not really slept soundly for days.

"To the drugstore. I have to leave a new prescription. They'll deliver it later."

"See here." I touched her coat. "I have to send my coat to the cleaners'. Let me borrow yours. I'm planning to go out, and I'll do your errand for you."

Irene glanced down, as if surprised to discover she was holding the coat. "This old thing—but you're all dressed up—" Then she brightened. "Would you really, Miss Jansen? I hate to leave Stuart. These colds of his are so bad. Maud has to stay with Aunt Elizabeth. There's no one to sit with Stuart while I'm gone. It's the drugstore right on the corner near the inn. Leave the prescription, and their boy will bring it up as soon as they have it ready. They're good about delivering. Sure—take my coat if you want."

She pushed the plaid horror at me and hurried up the stairs as if she feared I would change my mind. I shrugged the wrap on. I was near the same height as its owner, if, I thought smugly, a lot slimmer. Now I also had a legitimate excuse for leaving the house.

Pulling the hood up about my chin, I paused only to put on the boots I should have worn last night. There was a policeman outside, but on my producing the prescription he waved me on.

Around the corner would bring me to the carriage house by the way of Emma Horvath's drive. Ahead, I could see two men in uniform, moving people away from the front of another gate farther down. Behind them I caught a glimpse of the rear of an ambulance.

Why an ambulance? Surely no one had been hurt during our exercise in the garden last night. Unless—I stumbled.

The idea of what they might be dealing with made me a little sick. In the grave Miss Elizabeth had visited last night, there might already have been a burial. This was still murder—a murder which Miss Elizabeth had helped to conceal, by all I could guess.

I tramped up the Horvath drive, sure now I *was* going to leave the Abbey. If the police said "no"—at least I would have this day free.

Theodosia answered the door at once, ready with a spate of questions. Gordon Cantrell, his face pinched looking, as if he were beginning to shrivel into middle age without ever having fully matured, stared moodily into his coffee cup with the sullenness of a schoolboy who has been rated for some omission or commission. Yet there was no atmosphere of a recent quarrel. In fact, Theodosia appeared so intrigued by what was going on at the Abbey, she might have forgotten his presence. But I remembered, so I was not as frank as I might have been, giving only a slightly expanded version of what I had told Preston Donner.

"So that's what went on last night! Gordon went over and one of the police caught him and wanted to know what he was doing!"

"Stupid ass!" Gordon did not raise his eyes from his cup. "Had to hammer it into his thick skull. It wasn't until the other fellow came along he let me go. At least *he* had some sense."

"But it is all so unbelievable," Theodosia cut in. "If I wrote this into a book, the editor would make me yank it out as being too fantastic for any reader to swallow! I'd like to have Roger Whittleby here right now listening to this. Teach him to shake his head over manuscripts in the future. I wish I didn't have this foul deadline to meet. I'd take the day off and we'd have a good time chewing it over. No." She must have read the expression on my face. "It hasn't been any fun for you, or for the Austins, has it? I'm being cold-blooded again." She shot a glance at Gordon.

"You are." He struck in at her waspishly. But his wife paid no attention.

"Perhaps my attitude comes from dealing with murders by and gone. With those you can read the evidence in full, act as a biologist with strange insects to study. Somehow this Abbey affair does not seem real to me."

"Over here it doesn't." I agreed with her. Coming

into the carriage house had been walking out of an uncomfortable shadow into the light. "Over there, unfortunately it is. That is why I want to escape today—I need to get back a true perspective."

Gordon was glancing impatiently at his watch. But I was not going shopping in Irene's coat, and Theodosia agreed with me, producing a smart tan carcoat in its stead. Gordon stood near the outer door, by now drumming fingers on the edge of a briefcase. I wished I had thought of a taxi. Nor was our exit made any better when we had to wait for the police ambulance to pull out.

Had they discovered what they had been searching for? What grisly secret had been in the old burial plot?

"What's Rohmer doing working with the cops? I never heard of him joining up with the police before."

I blinked. "Rohmer? I haven't met any Rohmer at the Abbey." I thought I was entitled to hedge the truth that much. That abrupt scene last night had not been a real meeting. "It was a Lieutenant Daniels who seemed to be in charge—"

"Mark Rohmer was in the garden last night. And I'd like to know why. This isn't the sort of deal he's usually in on." When Gordon lapsed into silence, scowling at the windshield before him, I dared to pursue the subject.

"What does he do?"

"Oh, he's one of the hush-hush boys from Washington. He may be MI, or something like that. I wonder—" Gordon's scowl lightened a little. "Did they definitely identify that body as Roderick Frimsbee?"

"As far as I know."

"Then that may have brought Rohmer in. There were a lot of tales about Frimsbee some time back. Though I always thought he was a pretty small fish on the wrong side of the law. Unless he started moving into the big time lately."

"I heard that he had to go abroad to escape some kind of trouble here—"

"Too true. Drugs—though they could not get the connecting link to be more than suspicion at the time. He did something pretty raw, though the details never came out. I think if he'd stayed to hand he might have landed up in the pen sooner or later. The family can still swing enough weight—through Miss Emma and his mother knowing a few top brass in the Navy—so they got him out on bail. He skipped then, and I think the Austins were relieved in spite of the money loss. Then they said he was dead—maybe they hoped it. Yes, Roderick was a bad boy—a real black sheep." Gordon had regained some of his usual jauntiness. "But he must have outdone himself lately to bring Rohmer in."

"Then Mr. Rohmer *must* be important—" I could not stop, I wanted to know more—to hear all Gordon Cantrell could tell me. But he did not appear to think my interest out of the ordinary.

"He's a colonel now—but the word is that he deals with strictly top-level cases—things which have to be given the cover-up sometimes when there is a so-called sensitive angle. Yes, he's important. Pretty lone-wolf—I only got the word about him through a contact at the news center. He was pointed out to me there. Well." Gordon shrugged. "If this is the usual sort of case he handles we'll probably never know the inside story, close to it as we are. That is going to disappoint Theo."

He laughed. I did not like the harsh note in the laughter. It was plain that he was pleased at the thought his wife was going to be disappointed in something even so minor.

"I think," he continued, "I'm going to ask around a little, see what the official story is about Rohmer's being here. Rumors circulate, they always do."

There were more questions I would have liked to ask, but I knew the folly of pushing. The last thing I wanted was to arouse any interest in Gordon Cantrell, which could be turned in my direction so he would begin to wonder what tie I might have with Colonel Mark Rohmer.

"If Rohmer comes around asking questions, you had better be careful."

I was so startled by that I was afraid I had already betrayed too much interest.

"Why—why should I have anything to hide?"

"He's a fair-haired boy for some security department. And you've certainly heard what's gone on in that direction in the past."

I regained my composure. "You flatter me by thinking I have any deep, dark secrets to hide. And there is no reason why he would be at all interested in me. I had no contact at all with the Austins before last Saturday. And as soon as I can move I'll have no contact now either."

But Gordon might not have heard me. "I'd sure like

to know just what he's after at the Abbey." His voice plainly held an interrogative note.

Did Gordon expect me to provide him with reports of detection in progress? I could hardly accept that. But even as I speculated, his manner underwent a change, before my eyes he became another person. For the first time since our introduction I must be seeing the Gordon Cantrell Theodosia had seen when she married him. And, if the turning on of that charm had not been so calculated, I might have been moved by it. Once he must have played that role with conviction. Now his action creaked a little.

My first disgust became amusement. I relaxed to enjoy the show. He did not mention Mark again, but his reminder that tomorrow was Saturday, and why didn't I drop in in the evening, had the wrong touch. I thanked him for the lift, without agreeing or disagreeing with his invitation, as I got out of the car, took a deep breath of winter air, which, though tainted with exhaust fumes, was invigorating.

Holly wreaths hung in the windows; signs reminded one there remained just so many more days for Christmas shopping. For a moment I was troubled. Christmas is the day which is the hardest for those without families. We are told by psychiatrists and others dealing with our modern emotional ills that it is the season in which depression strikes the deepest for those prone to it, that grayest of ills. While Aunt Otilda's holiday celebrations, if one might term them that, had never been on the lavish side—far from it, indeed—the day had been sedately observed, with duties of cards written and strictly useful "gifts" exchanged. And this year I would not even be among the acquaintances I had had.

Nonsense—I needed shoes, not holly! I pushed by a bedroom-slipper display in the shop nearest the drugstore where I had dutifully left the prescription, and found a harried salesman. I came out of the shop a little later, rather exhausted.

There was a row of small specialty shops on a side street—the kind one always finds in a town of wealth, where the unusual and clever tempts a jaded shopper. Ladensville had been first a university town, and then subdivisions of one-of-a-kind suburban homes, of the class to tempt commuters from Washington, spread out over the old fields. The new subdivisions were still spreading, as I had seen when I came in on the bus from Washington on my arrival.

These shopwindows were showplaces for those luxuries which one of my training never has the courage to buy for herself. But when the holiday spirit strikes, one finds oneself making extravagant purchases for others.

A set of perfume bottles in the form of chessmen, a dragon pin with ruby eyes—those drew me from one window to the next. I began to feel the buying madness creeping on me. Something sobering was needed—perhaps a bookshop.

But before I reached the door above which a bookshop sign hung on a bracket, I had to pass an antique shop. There I paused before the fascinating display. A miniature eighteenth-century silver service was poised on a shelf, behind it a delicate fan of carved ivory and lace—

Winter street, the cloudy day, vanished as if a worn theater drop had been whisked upward out of sight. I stood now in sunlight, turning about in my fingers a small figure I had just picked up from a table of "white elephants" at a church bazaar, a figure which, to my certain knowledge, was now lying wrapped in an old handkerchief at the bottom of a drawer back in my Canton, New Hampshire, apartment. Yet here and now I saw its duplicate.

The sight of it jarred my new-found confidence, brought a stab of hurt. I would *not* think—

What had been the matter? That tiny spark I had never been wholly able to beat out flamed anew. Had I been so mistaken, in spite of my naivete? Had I indeed been as silly and stupid as I had named myself all these years? Or had I been just a little bit right—that there had been some depth below the surface? If I had only been able to ask that question and received an honest answer—it was not fair that one dared not throw away pride!

I forced myself to look beyond the figure which brought back memories. There was a snuffbox, a quaint old amethyst ring—its heart-shaped stone encircled by seed pearls. What did they say, in the old days, of the amethyst—that those wearing them could never become intoxicated? I should have had one on my finger five years ago. It was not fair! Though who said that anything in this world had to be fair? Only a child could cry out that when hurt.

Aunt Otilda had taken me young enough to shape me, make me eternally uncertain of emotion, mistrustful of it. By the time I was old enough to break loose I could not. I was secure only in her pattern—so stunted, warped, I was not a real woman at all—how could I be?

The wind found its way beneath the collar of Theodosia's coat. I shivered. Food—I needed warmth and food, and maybe to get away from this hateful town and humiliating memories which haunted it—and me. As I turned away from the window I bumped into a tall figure a little behind me.

I looked up without any real surprise. All the hours, the days, behind me had been really leading to this. I had to face matters and face them squarely at long last.

"Hello, Mark." Somehow I was strong enough to say that, as if we were only very casual acquaintances who had met only a short time ago.

"Christmas shopping?" He was as casual, and that strengthened me.

I tucked my package more firmly under my arm. "No—just new shoes—"

"As a result of your adventure last night?"

This was like another of my haunting dreams. Our meeting had had no proper beginning and would have no ending. Only when his hand touched my elbow, urging me lightly towards the building at my left, I obeyed. Nor did I find it strange to be in a restaurant, the hostess ushering us to a table.

Still enmeshed in that dream, I unbuttoned my coat, and answered the question he had asked on the street:

"Yes, I ruined my shoes last night—"

"Tell me—" He leaned forward. He was just the same—except for finger-wide strips of gray above his ears. I bit my lip. No! Not again, never again!

"What did you see in the garden?" he continued. His eyes did not quite reach mine. I forced my mind back to the here and now.

But I was so caught in that sensation of this being a dream that I lost all caution and told him the truth. "Miss Austin reading the burial service over an open grave. Emma Horvath's body was in that, wasn't it?"

"Yes." He picked up the menu and ordered swiftly as a waiter materialized at his elbow. He was remembering—no, it was simply chance, it had to be, that he picked out just those items.

I made a lengthy business of pulling off my gloves, tucking them into my purse. Anything seemed better than being silent and letting this unsteadiness build up inside me.

"But how did you come into the case?" I asked quickly.

"It's a long story."

"One you can't tell me!" I was glad to find even so slim a point on which I could begin to erect a new barrier of hostility.

"One which I am going to tell you here and now" was his reply.

8

So that was the real reason for our meeting! I snapped my purse shut on the gloves with a strong, if illogical, feeling of resentment. This was what I thought I had wanted—yet it hurt. No "It's been a long time, how have things been for you?"

Suppose I asked my own preferred question—"And how is Mrs. Rohmer?" But that was not allowed—by my pride.

"I know very little about any of this," I told him. "So I'd be grateful to hear what you have to say."

He seemed in no hurry to do that—even after stating so firmly that that was what he wanted.

"How did you come to be living there?" He shot the question as if hoping to startle some damaging reply out of me.

Once more I retraced the actions of Saturday night.

Was it only *last* Saturday that I had made my fatal mistake?

"So you see, I never saw any of them before. Of course I had heard of Dr. Austin's collection. Who in the literary world has not?"

Mark's dark face was as unreadable as ever, eyes upon me held a kind of contemptuous measurement— or was I being too sensitive and wary? I felt I was being assessed and weighed, and my irritation kindled anew. Nothing would ever break his calm. He was as polished and hard as Leslie Lowndes appeared on first acquaintance. Portrait of a soldier with not a single human chink in his battle armor.

"How much do you know about the family now?"

I recited tersely what Theodosia and Preston Donner had told me. Then, piqued by his armor, I added the shocking scene between Anne and Irene at the opening of the coffin. I hesitated for a moment. Miss Elizabeth—should I—

His level gaze caught and held mine. "That isn't all, is it?"

I reached for my glass of water, took a sip. That shaky feeling crept over me again. I could not dissemble—he would know—he did know.

"What happened last night?" He bore down with that demand as if he could reach into my mind and dig loose the thoughts I found hard now to discipline.

"Mark—"

"It's Miss Elizabeth, isn't it? Did you follow her?"

"How did you—did you see her, too?" Something of the weight rolled from me at his words.

"Yes. She must have known about the substitution

near when it occurred, of course. The why she kept quiet is what is important." He fell silent as our waiter produced salads and a basket of hot rolls.

I relaxed a little more. "I don't know why, honestly. What is at the bottom of it all, do you know, Mark?"

"We can guess—a little—enough to start working on. Your informants were right on one heading. Roderick was the Austin black sheep. From all accounts he was one of those egotists who slip easily onto the wrong side of the law because when they want a thing they see no reason why they shouldn't have it. Money—women—and if anyone gets hurt in the process that's nothing to people like him.

"Sometimes they get away with it, staying just inside the law so that they can't be nailed for anything, no matter how many lives they wreck. But sooner or later most of them slide across that barrier they do not think exists—for them. Roderick skipped the bail Mrs. Horvath put up to save the family's face. He was reported killed. Instead he was making new contacts and much stronger ones. We had news of him from Interpol— that he was connected—slightly—with another case. He had a tail on him in New York—a week ago he slipped our man and disappeared. But we hoped he might show up here. And you are sure you saw him in the garden Saturday night?"

"I didn't have more than a quick glimpse, but that uniform coat—I couldn't be wrong about that. Where could he have gotten it?"

"Out of the wardrobe in the playhouse," Mark replied absently. He poked at a sliding piece of lettuce. "The outer door had been forced and we found his other clothing there. He must have arranged a meeting with someone—"

"Who?"

For the first time Mark smiled. I looked away hastily. I wanted him to keep to his question-and-answer game, and strictly away from any personalities.

"That's something we need answered. It's an odd company there in the house. There are the remaining Austin sisters—Miss Elizabeth—who seems to have made such an impression on you. You do like her, don't you? But then you are conditioned to respond to her type. How *is* Aunt Otilda, by the way?" I heard the mockery he did not try in any way to conceal.

"She died two years ago. Yes, I like Miss Elizabeth. If she has any secrets, I don't think they are for her own benefit."

"I think I am inclined to agree with you there. But she does have a lot to account for. Then there's Mrs. Anne Frimsbee who, I gather, you do not care for—"

I moved uncomfortably. Had I pressed judgment where my opinions could do the most harm?

"Only my personal reaction," I said quickly. "One does take dislikes, sometimes quite without reason. She was terribly shocked and upset in the parlor. I can understand why she did not want anyone to know Roderick's identity. She must have been very badly hurt by him in the past."

"But—you don't like her. Mrs. Irene Frimsbee you seem to be uncertain about. Why? She didn't provoke that scene. And since then, according to you, she has effaced herself. Why are you equivocal about her?"

I flushed and hoped my discomfort was not too apparent. He had read a good deal, perhaps from my tone of voice. Because of his insistence, I was forced to think more of my attitude towards Irene Frimsbee. It was my own hurt which might have awakened my distrust. I would not tell the truth—that I had seen Irene in close conversation at the Humbolt with a man certainly not her husband—and that had recalled too much of my own troubles in the past.

"I wasn't aware of any bias," I said flatly. I would stand firm on that.

"And how does Miss Lowndes impress you?" Apparently he was willing to forego any more probing along the Frimsbee line.

"I think she is a very efficient person."

"She is having an affair with Cantrell," he returned impersonally. He might have been commenting on the toughness of the steak.

"I know nothing about that."

Once more he did not comment, but continued his own appraisal of the household.

"Preston Donner has an excellent reputation in his field. He was associated with Dr. Austin—did book-hunting for him. There were rumors ten years back that he wanted to marry Miss Elizabeth—"

"But—" I interrupted, now a little shocked, "she must be years older—"

"Not so much as you would think. Donner is into his sixties, even if he is well preserved, as they used to say. He is an advisor now, for the purchase of any new items for the Austin collection. You know that the good doctor left most of his cash to be kept in trust for just that purpose. Mrs. Horvath was the final judge for what would be bought. I don't know who will take over her duties now. Seems Dr. Edward thought Emma had a shrewd head on her shoulders when it came to money. She did have some control of the Horvath holdings and managed well.

"Then there's Hanno Horvath, Mrs. Emma's nephew by marriage. He got a small trust fund from his uncle's estate—but again Mrs. Emma had the final say-so over his expenditures."

"I've seen very little of Mr. Horvath. I believe he teaches literature at the university."

"He's an associate professor, yes. And it was he who introduced Miss Lowndes to the household. Their relationship is on another basis now, of course. Oddly enough, Horvath seems to have expressed no rancor over being replaced in that lady's affections. All in all—" Mark was being judicial now, a phase of his character which I had never cared much for. "There are some very interesting sources for friction within those walls."

I thought it time to gain some information in return. "What was Roderick doing that he had to be tailed?"

"It was rather what he might be going to do. We have reason to believe that he was involved in a case which has baffled us for some time—the laundry business—"

"What?" I was completely startled. Mark laughed.

"Nothing to do with soap and water. The laundering of money, hot money from robberies and illicit gambling, drugs—taken overseas, used to purchase anything worthwhile up for sale. Antiques, perhaps. Which could then be sold openly here. If Dr. Austin were still

SNOW SHADOW **123**

alive we could be more certain. As it is we can only guess. Mrs. Horvath had a part in the set-up—not perhaps knowingly—but she kept a tight pocketbook, and she knew the value of a bargain. However, in these security-conscious days you have to dig for information, even from your supposed teammates. This situation." He shook his head. "It looks as if it was getting out of hand. I need a contact inside—"

Inside. I smiled wryly. Contact with the Abbey, a bargain-counter Mata Hari—for him. It was a part of what I had discovered about Mark Rohmer—the man who would play all the angles—

"The racket," he continued, "is a big one. We know it has overseas ties. And it spreads into places we cannot probe without gold-plated evidence. So we've had to move slowly. Roderick was a lead, and we lost him just perhaps when he was about to pay off.

"There is a ring of what you might term 'importers' around the world. Old families ruined by war, or revolution, or confiscatory taxes, are willing to part with treasures for cash, pieces collectors could never hope to see appear normally on the market. And they aren't—on the open market, that is. Sales are private—income-tax collectors and official snoopers are left in the dark. The sellers get the cash which is so 'laundered,' and the other sales are made here. Of course there is a profit, too. And the go-betweens get a cut. But no one has to answer embarrassing questions.

"The American who wants to sink some unreported income in a hedge against inflation makes his deal with the ring and acquires a bargain which is tax free. He may have to keep it in hiding—but he has it. So far the scheme works. Unfortunately, some time ago the ring discovered that the supply of family treasures is beginning to dry up. And there are other problems—some of our none-too-good political friends have found this a promising way to get dollars dubiously. So now the ring—or a portion of it—has moved on from the dirty-money boys into another business. Their answer is fakes—fakes which are very close to perfect. Of course, there is some conflict in the ring itself now—the dirty-money dealers are not too pleased with a change which doesn't solve their problem."

"What kind of fakes?"

"Very clever forgeries—done by masters in the business. The ring is protected in these cases because the buyer cannot display his recent acquisition. He has to salt it away. So the fake may not be discovered for years. And the friends of art behind the Iron and Bamboo Curtains have quite a few models for the fakers. Take the recent tomb discoveries in China—some fascinating articles can be offered with the suggestion that they were stolen on the sites by an enterprising opponent of Mao, who subsequently escaped to Hong Kong. So it can be set up almost anywhere there is the rare material for the fakers.

"The lid blew off for us about six months ago when Homer Blackwell died."

"Blackwell—oh, he was that oil man the Treasury Department was trying to indict for tax evasion." A memory of newspaper headlines came to me.

"Yes. He was killed in a plane crash on his way to Washington. He had a collection of ceramics which had to be appraised for the estate. Among his ceramics was a Ming horse—which wasn't appraised. So now we are hunting for a corporation milking this country for cash. And some of it is sent elsewhere to make up payrolls which we want to stop."

"How do the Austins figure in this?"

"Through the doctor's trust. Most of what was left of his wife's fortune is in that. He wanted his library to be the best."

"But I don't see—there are no Austin items worth forging—"

"What could exist in Austeniana which would be worth a lot of hard cash *if* they might be found to exist?"

I considered. "Several things. The letters that Jane's sister Cassandra is known to have burned, especially if they prove that Jane did have the much-speculated-upon romance in Devonshire which is thought to have inspired *Persuasion*. The first draft of *Pride and Prejudice*—the one she entitled *First Impressions* and later rewrote. Or the corresponding first version of *Sense and Sensibility*, which was called *Elinor and Marianna*. But all of those were known to have been destroyed— and anyway they would not be as great a treasure as to bring prices worth faking for—"

"Except," Mark reminded me, "from someone like the doctor who was obsessed with the subject, and left a will directing such purchases. Also, can one be entirely certain that everything was destroyed? Remember how they discovered all the Boswell material in an Irish castle? Papers do come to light mysteriously sometimes. And we can be sure that when this firm deals in anything it has a well-documented and plausible pedigree."

"But Dr. Austin is dead. Rather late to attempt a sale now, no matter what the trust was intended for."

"Not so. The dream of the Austin library did not die with him—he made it very clear that Mrs. Emma was to see it was carried out. Preston Donner was to vet anything bought."

"Did Emma Horvath have a real interest in the library?"

"She had an interest in the prestige of the Austin family. Someone could play on that. Emma Horvath had money, but she was trying to gain the entry into the kind of society which does not think too much of money—more of personalities. She resented Miss Elizabeth's status here in Ladensville. A Horvath simply does not rate beside an Austin.

"Two months ago Mrs. Horvath arranged to liquidate some stocks—about a hundred thousand dollars' worth. The liquidation was still in process when she had the fall and broke her hip."

"What does Mr. Donner have to say?"

"He denies knowledge of anything having been offered to her. But suppose she was approached through Roderick."

"Would she listen to him? He'd skipped bail and she lost the money she put up for that."

Mark shrugged. "Who knows? She might have had a liking for him still. He had charm—and she wouldn't be the first lady of her age to be influenced by that. In fact she had something of a reputation that way. He had a name for squiring the older generation while he was abroad."

"But now she is dead." Suddenly a new thought struck me. "How did she die?"

"A guess?" He looked amused. "Yes, now we are concerned with that. Her doctor, after official inquiry, was disturbed. He had tried to talk Miss Elizabeth into an autopsy. At that time she refused; since he had only vague suspicions he could not push it. Now it is a police matter."

"But why—if she were going to buy— *Oh!*" Again I thought I could guess. "There might be those who would object to such a sum of money going out of the family—*was* it her money?"

"No. It was the last of the Austin estate, as far as we have been able to discover. And to pay that much for some sheets of paper, no matter what was written on them—yes, there could be objections to that. Especially when there was a chance that the trust will naturally otherwise come to an end in a year's time. It was only to hold for twenty years.

"Horvath's her heir. She had only life interest in her husband's estate. The rest, her personal holdings, will be divided between Miss Austin and her nephew Charles. That remainder might be sizable. Mrs. Emma was a good businesswoman. Her will was made years ago when she was left trustee. But there have been rumors that she was thinking of revising it."

The matter seemed bleakly plain. Miss Austin struggling to keep up the house with limited funds, Charles Frimsbee, now an invalid, both needing money badly.

"What about Charles Frimsbee?"

Mark shook his head. "He's the only one with an absolutely airtight alibi for anything. The poor fellow had a third operation last week. He's been in the hospital since they released him as a POW from Vietnam. But there's his wife—"

"But you are not sure there was anything wrong with Mrs. Horvath's death. And Roderick might have been killed by someone with no connection with the family at all!"

"I am afraid that would be overly optimistic."

I was back in the place where the past and present revolved dizzily together.

"So you want me to watch the suspects for you? How did you know where I was today?"

"You were followed."

"I should have invited my 'tail' to share a taxi, then," I flared. "And I have no talent for spying! What right—"

"Have I to ask you to do so?" he finished.

"Yes, what indeed?"

"Someday—" His face was unreadable, and chilled me by its closed-in quality, its lack of expression. "We shall have some explanations. In the meantime—yes, I have no right to ask this of you. I'm on a job. I was called in because of Roderick. I will not meddle at all if this proves to be a routine crime investigation, but I have a hunch. Sometimes one develops a sixth sense."

I nodded.

"I honestly believe, Erica, that the murderer of Roderick Frimsbee is now living in the Abbey. And I think that uncovering of what lies behind all this is important. You can refuse to help, however, if you wish."

For a long moment I looked down at the tablecloth, seeing neither the fabric nor our dishes. He was deadly serious about this. If I had become another and wiser person, as I had hoped, this was a chance to prove it.

"All right. What must I do?"

"Gordon Cantrell is the only one, other than the police and you, who knows that I was at the Abbey last night. It was pure bad luck running into him. He will have to be satisfied with a story—"

"I don't know how!" My protest was swift. I might be a writer of creative fiction, but this baffled me.

"Just back me up. You have only to go along with it." He looked at his watch. "Do you have any more shopping?"

"No. The shoes are all I really needed. And I mostly wanted to get out of the Abbey."

"Good enough. I'll drive you to the Cantrells'. You introduce me to Mrs. Cantrell—I met you—we discussed last night—enough for a social contact."

I could not find any ready excuse. Obediently I arose from the table, slipped into the coat he held ready. A black car had pulled to the curb outside. The driver got out and Mark took his place.

"Back by six," he told the other.

Our talk, as he drove, was not polite chatter. To my surprise, Mark spoke of my book as if he had read it—though I would hardly think it would be of interest to him. He asked about the research I was now doing, and I outlined the task before me. But both of us avoided the "do-you-remembers" which might have been normal.

As we came into the street of the Horvath house I

saw that the gate leading to the theater was closed, the police cars gone. We pulled into the courtyard of the carriage house, I was out quickly, reaching for the knocker before Mark caught up. I wanted to get this over quickly.

Theodosia opened the door, and I introduced my companion with a steady voice. She welcomed us as if she had been hoping for such an interruption.

"I don't know whether you are aware of it or not, Colonel Rohmer, but writers live on coffee when in the throes of work, and I have a pot on the boil now. Sit down and share it, both of you."

I was content to sip my coffee, leaving conversation to them. They got along well. Mark engaged in easy shop talk. I wondered how much homework he had put in learning the fields of interest of those he needed to contact. Now he was deep in the Kitteridge case with Theodosia.

My watch marked three-thirty, and I knew, without being told, Mark wanted to stay until Gordon arrived. But that might not be for hours! I heard him skillfully guiding the talk to the Abbey and Theodosia holding forth on the fantastic truth which would not be allowed in fiction.

Mark's charm was not surface-obvious as was Gordon's, nor had it become threadbare over the passing years. I felt the old pull and kept reminding myself that there were darker sides to his nature. He could be as cruel as his Blackfoot ancestors had once been said to be.

It had never bothered me that Mark was Indian. In fact, that had added to his attraction. Though education and wide travel had divorced him from what one might expect of his race, yet I was sure under that outer shell he must be governed by the mores of another people.

"Theo!" The front door opened and there sounded the bellow of a thoroughly exasperated man. "Who in the hell parked that car so I can't pull in?"

Mark arose with that feline grace of movement particularly his. Theodosia was clearly annoyed.

"Gordon, we have guests! Come in—"

Gordon appeared in the doorway. He did not even blink when he saw the guests, or at least one of them.

We were all very polite, exchanging neat platitudes for the next few minutes. But I knew Theodosia was irked. I wondered then if she knew what Mark had told me about Gordon and Leslie. Gordon's attitude might be termed wary.

I was reluctant to end the scene, though I refused to analyze why. Mark glanced at his watch, but he lingered—as if he were setting the stage for some future role.

When he finally left, Theodosia spoke first:

"Where did you meet him?"

Remembering my pretense of ignorance with Gordon, I had to be wary.

"Last night—he's the one who chased me. We ran into each other in town and he wanted to apologize today about that. Now—I must go. Bucking the shopping crowds was something. I'm going back and put my feet up. Thanks for the coffee and the loan of the coat."

Theodosia smiled. Another time that knowing look

would have made me squirm. But suddenly I *was* tired, as if I had been under a strain which had drained my energy. I put on Irene's coat and walked back across the garden.

A car was pulling up under the portico. Its license plate bore the green seal of a doctor.

Miss Elizabeth—had she taken a turn for the worse? I hurried in—yet I wanted no more Austin burdens, only the peace and quiet to be found in my room.

9

As I climbed the stairs I heard voices and in the upper hall I came face to face with Irene and the doctor. Since our meeting in the morning, the younger Mrs. Frimsbee's appearance had deteriorated even more. Lacking makeup, her face had an unhealthy gray look and there were brown stains under her eyes. She pushed at loose ends of hair impatiently and about her mouth were brackets of mulish stubbornness.

"—not there," she was saying. "He's too little, he wouldn't understand. They don't really care—with them it's all routine and efficiency. He'd be frightened to death. And surely he can't be *that* sick!"

"Under the circumstances," the doctor cut in, "I would seriously consider it, Mrs. Frimsbee. It is very easy for such a condition to slip into pneumonia."

Irene shook her head. "I have the vaporizer and you

gave him the shots. He'll be all right, I know he will! Stuart is not going to any hospital!" She spat out the last word as if it were loathsome.

The doctor shrugged. "I haven't been able to locate a nurse to help you here—"

"I don't need one, I know how to take care of my own child! Goodness knows, Stuart's had enough colds in the past."

"This may be more than a cold before we are through, Mrs. Frimsbee. If there is any change, if he starts the heavy coughing again, call me at once."

Irene, one hand on the knob of her bedroom door, plainly begrudged the time spent in listening to such admonitions.

"He's calling me now. Stuart doesn't want anyone but me. A strange nurse would only frighten him. If I took him to the hospital, he would be scared to death. Ever since Aunt Emma yelled at him that time—" Her lips twisted. "Thank you for coming, Doctor. I'll be in touch." She went in, closing the door firmly behind her.

The doctor uttered an annoyed exclamation and I asked:

"Is the child seriously ill?"

"A bad case of bronchial virus. She should have him in the hospital. If you can influence Mrs. Frimsbee to understand that, you would be doing them both a favor. Hello, Maud." The maid had materialized like an apparition out of the wall.

"Doctor, can you come to Miss Elizabeth? She's greatly disturbed."

"As who wouldn't be in this house now!" the doctor

exploded. "I'd like to pack her off, too. All this commotion isn't doing that heart of hers any good. Well, let's see what can be done."

With a feeling of guilt I could not account for, I trailed the other two down the hall. This was repeating something—Aunt Otilda! In her last year she had depended upon me so much that even a necessary shopping trip, demanding only a short absence, was enough to thoroughly upset her for the rest of the day. But *I* was in no way responsible for Miss Elizabeth.

I could hear Miss Elizabeth's voice—muffled but raised in uncharacteristic argument. Was Mrs. Anne in there? But surely Maud would not have then left her charge. The voice went on and on, seeming to repeat the same words. Then I knew she must be talking to herself, or to shadows she alone saw. My suspicion was confirmed when Maud, sighting me, stepped before the door to bar my way.

"Is there any way I can help?"

"Thank you, no, miss. Miss Elizabeth is wandering-like. We'll see to her." Maud eyed me warily as if she expected me to try to push by, intrude on her mistress. I nodded and turned away.

However, I was not to find in my room the haven I sought. On the hearth were the ashes of a burned-out fire, some puffed onto the edge of the carpet. Though the bed had been made, missing was that aura of good housekeeping which had been so noticeable before.

At the side window which overlooked the garden, the shade was askew as if someone had had an observation post there. Balanced on the sill was an ashtray containing three crushed-out cigarettes. Someone *had* stood here, long enough to smoke three cigarettes. Irene? Anne? Leslie?

Angrily I dumped the contents of the tray into a piece of paper, folded that into a tight packet for the wastebasket. I sniffed the air resignedly. Being allergic to smoke, I would have to air out the room or expect a headache. I opened the window.

There was nothing to be seen in the garden. I tried to locate the burial ground and the theater. The line of dark yews walling in the first was all which could be sighted. And only the roof of the latter could be marked. Had the watcher here been spying on the police activity of the morning?

I shivered with more than the chill of the open window. Had that watcher been regretting a ruined plan?

It had been a recklessly daring plan—spoiled by Anne's insistence upon the coffin being opened. Therefore, Anne herself could not have been responsible for the substitution. As if she could have had anything to do with the murder of her own son!

I closed the window, dropped into the wing chair by the fireplace and tried to think. Other things—mainly memories—kept getting in the way.

We are molded by our environment in childhood. If nothing forces us to break those early patterns, we continue our lives within their limits. In basic matters I could only judge the motives and actions of others by those standards drilled into me. But because my training would not allow this or that derivation from the rules, it did not mean others were so monitored.

Actions which appeared to me without sensible motivation might be entirely necessary to those involved.

How could I judge anyone under this roof? Not by my standards of conduct anyway.

I had come to know—without the strength to alter them—that some of my rules were awry in this modern world. This led me to deceive myself concerning the actions of others. During the past few hours the thin shell, resulting from years of repression and self-discipline, had cracked, leaving me afraid and defenseless.

There was no escape from seeing Mark again, save flight for a second time. That was out of the question. I must reconstruct my armor. My fingers twisted together until I was dimly aware of pain. I must *not* let my thinking always circle back to Mark! That door was closed—must be kept so.

Not Mark—but murder. Only, that violent act seemed unreal, having little to do with me. Murder was something which happened in books or you read about with distaste in the newspapers. It did not engulf the ordinary people one meets and talks with, occur in a house in which one actually lives!

Irene, Anne, Leslie—I knew only what I had gained from surface impressions. By all the rules of justice I must make no assumptions.

Irene had good reason to hate Emma Horvath. But what possible reason could move her to kill a long-missing brother-in-law? If a woman had been connected with this crime, she must have a male confederate. Otherwise the exchange of bodies would have been impossible. Irene was small, giving no impression of strength. Her mother-in-law was even less robust.

It would be easy to nominate Leslie to head the list of suspects. She represented all I disliked in my own sex. Only there was no possible motive, no link with Roderick. If it had not been for those cigarettes—

Pain stabbed above my eyes. Either I had not aired the room long enough, or my nerves were attacking. I hunted out the tablets which would stop the headache, but I needed water to wash them down.

Which meant descent to the kitchen. I found the cook was not alone, though she occupied her rocking chair, staring out of the window with the air of one divorcing herself from the activity behind her. The reason for her withdrawal was at the stove, fussing with a small saucepan.

Anne Frimsbee had again applied the amount of makeup she had worn on her arrival, but not to such lacquered results. She frowned with irritation as she twisted the pan back and forth. But, to my surprise, she gave me a sourish smile.

"Some gruel for Stuart—" She moved the saucepan an inch to the right. "When Charles was small he thought only I could make gruel. He used to have these same heavy colds." She shook her head, but this show of maternal concern did not fit her. The picture of an anxious grandmother brewing a potion for her grandson was not really in focus.

"A cup of tea." She abandoned the gruel and spoke to me. "A cup of tea is so refreshing, don't you agree, Miss Jansen? Will you join me in having one?"

I could not refuse, though neither Mrs. Frimsbee's fussing, not the brooding Reena, made me want to stay in the kitchen.

Anne Frimsbee did not consult the silent presence in the bay window, but proceeded to search through cupboards until she lined up cups and saucers, a tea kettle, a box of tea bags, and had put water on to boil. Her exploration of a breadbox led to the appearance of some crumbling odds and ends of sweet rolls, and a snort from Reena, which Anne deliberately ignored, as she assembled all her finds on a tray.

"We can go into the breakfast room. I'll just wait until the water boils—"

I carried the tray. The room had an air of neglect I could not associate with Miss Elizabeth's house. Rumpled and strewn with crumbs, the tablecloth had not been changed. I set down the tray and went to look out to the garden.

"Very dreary now," Anne commented as she hurried in. "But in summer it is really quite pleasant. My sister is an enthusiastic gardener, and she carried out Father's plan of an Austen garden in great detail."

"An Austen garden?"

"An arrangement of all the flowers and shrubs which would have been in Jane Austen's own garden. Of course, lately Elizabeth has not had the time to care for it properly. Most of the bushes should have been pruned, and the wisteria down at the arbor is quite out of control. But I must admit that the delphiniums made a pure wall of color last year. Very noticeable. A photographer came from some garden magazine to take a picture."

"I never heard of an Austen garden before."

"Oh, Father's interests spread beyond just Miss Austen's works. That was what he insisted we call her— 'Miss Austen.' He said she would have been appalled to know that 'Jane' was familiarly used by strangers.

Father always believed that Austin and Austen had a common beginning and we could claim kin. The money he spent on genealogical research trying to prove that!" Anne Frimsbee came back to the table. "Father's enthusiasms ran very deep, and were not confined to the books. There was the year he concentrated on the theater. That was a very gay time. They presented *Pride and Prejudice* and were in rehearsal for *Persuasion*—" She paused to pour hot water into a flowered cup with care, drop in a tea bag. "I was disappointed when it was not given."

"Why wasn't it?"

"We were lacking a Captain Wentworth on opening night." Anne's lips set under their coating of paint. She might have been one of Aunt Otilda's generation deploring a moral lapse. "My sister Elinor—of course she had always been too restricted, Father had some very old-fashioned ideas about what was becoming for a daughter—and Elinor, poor thing, never knew how to handle Father. He could be most charming when one approached him properly. Elinor was such an intense girl—I think she got on Father's nerves—demanding, mind you demanding—to be sent to college and the like. Father was extremely upset.

"Well, Elinor eloped with the young actor who was to play Captain Wentworth. He was very handsome and in that uniform—"

Her spat of reminiscence came to an abrupt end. Was it that uniform in which Roderick had been found? I glanced up and caught a sly, measuring look, veiled in the instant her eyes met mine. Why was all this family history being poured out with the tea?

"Naturally Father was furious and we never heard from Elinor again," she swept on, "It was very sad and upsetting. Father was more strict with all of us after that. He closed the theater at once, and everything was put away. Though the play had been quite well received, written up in newspapers and magazines."

She was ignoring that the theater must have been used by Roderick for a shelter. By her present attitude, one might believe that Roderick Frimsbee had never existed. Was this her escape from unpleasant fact?

"I think that it was Elinor's elopement which made Father really eccentric. He became quite a recluse before his death. Only Preston Donner saw him during the whole year before he died. Even Elizabeth had to talk to him through the door. And he cared less and less for the family. It was his wish to establish the Austin Library as a gift to the university. He admired Emma's business sense—she was like him in some ways. She always knew just what she wanted and went after it. Money *does* make a vast difference in one's view of life. Don't you agree, Miss Jansen?"

I swallowed a bite of stale bun to answer.

"Never having had very much that I did not earn, I can't pretend to be an authority on the subject."

"Yes, and a government pension doesn't lead to expanded ideas either." Her statement was acid. "Emma married Alexis Horvath when she was eighteen. But she didn't get what she expected, not for quite a while. Alexis had old-fashioned ideas about women, and he held the purse strings—tight. But Emma worked out her own arrangements after a bit and she was quite comfortable. She had stores charge things she didn't buy, and collected the money after Alexis paid the bills. I don't think he ever discovered she was playing the market. Emma was one of the few people who sold out before the Twenty-Nine Crash. She seemed to have a sixth sense about money. Of course, she was only left life interest in the Hovarth estate.

"Hanno will get that now. He is the only son of Alexis' younger brother. But there's Emma's own money, and Charles always was her favorite." Anne was foreseeing a rosy future.

But what, I mused, about the recent break between Irene and Miss Emma? The will was an old one, Mark had said. Emma Horvath might just have left a more recent one.

"Yes, Charles was always her favorite," Anne repeated happily. "Though she was always close-mouthed, her personal estate must be more than comfortable. Father came to rely on her judgment in financial matters. He made her the major trustee of the library fund."

"Did she buy much for that?" Perhaps Anne Frimsbee might have heard a rumor about a manuscript.

"Nothing so far. Though Emma was very mysterious just before she had her accident. She hinted about some unusual business deal. I've been in Forida with my mother-in-law—she's the widow of Admiral Quinton Frimsbee, you know, a sweet woman. Invited me to spend the winter with her. Then these old friends of hers took a place in the Bahamas and asked her over. She thought it was such a wonderful chance to see her daughter—Lucile married a British officer during the war and he's on some kind of official business there. I offered to stay and keep the cottage open, but Angela wouldn't hear of it, said she didn't expect me to assume such responsibility. Though it really wouldn't have been any trouble at all—and I do feel these damp Maryland winters so much. But Angela's quite a decisive person—rather like Emma."

And you hate her insides, I deduced, just as you must have hated Emma. That poisonously sweet tone gives it away.

Spite was strong in Anne Frimsbee. It dripped in corrosive acid from her speech, shone out of her heavily madeup eyes, deepened the brackets about her mouth. No wonder Mrs. Admiral Frimsbee had gone off to the Bahamas after some weeks of her dear daughter-in-law's company.

I bet you make Irene jump through hoops, too, I added silently as I gulped a last mouthful of tea, anxious to get away. But I was not to escape so easily, for the door to the hall opened and Leslie Lowndes came in, flying flags of anger in her hot eyes and flushed cheeks.

"I want to know," she demanded, "just what has gone on here. Why should that stupid detective come to my office for a second time and order me back here with him? What is the matter? Who's dead now?"

There was a crash of china. From the pieces of Anne's cup, a puddle of tea spread over the carpet. Seeing the white and naked terror in her face, I knew that all the babble of the last half-hour had been only a defense. Mrs. Frimsbee, a badly shaken woman, sat staring at Leslie as if the other had thrown a snake onto the table.

"Nothing has happened as far as we know," I answered.

Leslie sat down and took out a cigarette case. With quick, nervous fingers she chose one and lit it, narrowing her eyes and fanning the smoke away from her face.

"Something must have blown up. A neutron bomb, by the way the police are acting. I think we are in for another session of Truth or Consequences. Odd you haven't heard anything, though—"

Or have you? Her eyes accused us both. Anne Frimsbee was mopping at the tea with a wad of Kleenex. I edged back from the trails of cigarette smoke.

"I'm getting very tired of all this," Leslie continued crisply.

"But nothing has happened, nothing at all!" Anne's voice was shrill. I thought she might be close to tears and hysteria. "Why don't they let us alone? It isn't fair—it isn't! I'm not going to answer any more questions!" She threw the sodden paper wad onto the tea tray and stood up. "I'm going to my room," she announced, "and I'm not coming down here again—to talk to the police or anyone else!"

She scuttled out. Leslie laughed. "A neat trick if she can pull it off. The police have been handling the family carefully so far. This may be the day when the gloves will come off. Roderick was a thoroughly bad hat. None of them are able to deny that—nor pretend that he just doesn't exist—which they would like to."

She sounded so emphatic that I asked without thinking, "Did you know him?" I expected a negative reply, but, to my surprise, Leslie nodded.

"Yes. Though I had really forgotten about him—until they showed me the body. I met him once in Washington—before he skipped overseas. It was at one of those parties where no one seems to know the hostess and nearly everybody drifts in with a friend or two. Shortly after that, he got tagged for one of his deals. And were they deals! That will all be dragged up now that he's dead—in this way. I feel sorry for Miss Elizabeth—she's had enough to worry her. Anne and the rest can take their chances—but she's borne the brunt of all the past troubles."

"Any disgrace will hit her hard."

Leslie shrugged. "Sure. But there's nothing to be done about it. Lots of old families produce a rotten branch or two on the family tree. The Austins aren't unique in that. Well, here's my faithful boy in blue. Which one to the torture chamber this time?"

Sergeant Blake stood in the doorway. But it was to me he beckoned. Bewildered and a little apprehensive, I followed him to the library. Really, I thought, Lieutenant Daniels ought to begin paying Miss Elizabeth rent for the use of the room. But Daniels was not alone. Mark sat there also, a very grim line about his mouth.

He, rather than Daniels, spoke first.

"This goes deeper than we thought, Erica. Mrs. Horvath was poisoned."

"Poisoned?" I echoed.

"Yes." Daniels pushed towards me a tin box, patterned in a blue and gold pseudo-Oriental design. "Have you ever seen this before?"

10

Without thinking, I put out my hand, but, before my fingers closed on the box, I hesitated. There were no objections, so I picked it up.

"I have one like this at home, only it is red and gold. It was a gift container for a special brand of tea. They are not uncommon. Especially around holiday time."

"This one had candied ginger in it," Daniels said. Then he continued. "Have you seen one like it here?"

I shook my head. "I have only been in the kitchen twice. I have never looked in the cupboards, and the tea I saw this afternoon was in bags. No ginger—"

"But," Mark said, "isn't candied ginger a confection? Would it be used in cooking?"

Now I had the authority of the better informed. "Ginger is used in cooking. It has to be grated or

149

shredded for a garnish on icing—sliced thin and used in the tea instead of lemon. People also eat it like candy, though it is pretty hot."

"Hmm—" The lieutenant looked as if I had provided him with new ideas. "Then you might find it in any kitchen?"

"I think so, if the cook was imaginative."

"How long does it keep, once the tin is opened?" was Mark's next question.

"With a lid firmly on the tin between uses, indefinitely. It is preserved. But I don't understand—" I glanced from one man to the other.

"Very simple." Again it was Mark who replied. "This particular ginger has had something else added."

I put the tin down hastily. "Poison?"

"Poison," he confirmed. "It seems that—" he began, when Daniels cut in:

"You never met Mrs. Horvath?"

"No. She had her accident long before I came. I heard that Miss Austin and Irene Frimsbee visited her. I think they did last Sunday, and she was better."

"Did Mrs. Horvath like preserved ginger?"

"I don't know. No one mentioned that."

"And you have never seen such a container as this?"

"If it was supposed to be here before Mrs. Horvath's death," I retorted, "I wouldn't have had much chance to. I moved in last Sunday, and shortly after left with Mrs. Cantrell. During the time between arriving and leaving again, I did not visit the kitchen, nor did I see such a box. I doubt I would have noticed it anyway unless my attention had been called to it."

Daniels rubbed one finger along his jaw and Mark's

eyes were half-closed, an indication, I knew of old, that he was thinking. Was my inquisition over now? But Mark had one last question:

"Do you happen to know if anyone in the house is a gardener?"

"Mrs. Anne Frimsbee said that Miss Austin had created an Austen garden. The delphiniums were noted—"

"Delphiniums!" Daniels was a cat pouncing on a long-expected mouse. "There are delphiniums here?"

"According to Mrs. Frimsbee they are quite famous. Some garden magazine sent a photographer here to take pictures of them. But I don't see—"

"Did you ever hear of staphisagriae semina?" Daniels pronounced the words with such care I judged he had not heard of them often himself.

"No. Is it a poison?"

"The ripe seeds of a certain type of delphinium," Mark supplied.

The look Daniels gave him was not one of unqualified approval. Perhaps the Lieutenant had not intended to share that information.

"Anyone besides Miss Austin work in the garden? She's pretty old to do heavy work now—"

"They all may take turns, for all I know." I was growing impatient. "I haven't exchanged many confidences. I'm afraid I'm of small help to you."

"But you can be, Miss Jansen." That was Daniels. "We have been repeatedly told that Miss Austin is too ill to see us. Short of battering down her door, we can't make headway. Will you look in on her and give us a clear and unbiased report on her condition?"

He had trapped me. I could not refuse without arousing his suspicions, perhaps focusing them even more strongly on Miss Elizabeth.

"I will do what I can." I was not going to be too quick with any affirmative answer. "Are you through with me now?"

"Yes. And thank you very much, Miss Jansen." He placed the ginger tin back in the center of the desk, where the attention of his next victim would be unerringly drawn to it.

Mark escorted me to the door. "Do your best with Miss Austin. It will be better for her to let us get to the bottom of this as quickly as possible."

I hoped he was right. So Miss Elizabeth was not one of their prime suspects? However, I did not believe that that fact was going to make the interrogation easier for the woman upstairs.

As I went I tried to think how I could warn her. To get past Maud would be difficult. Then—what could I say? "Miss Austin, you had better tell the police all your secrets?"

Miss Elizabeth, safely ill in her room, could keep the police dangling as long as she wished. The Austin name still counted for something in Ladensville. A few words from her doctor might hold the authorities at bay. Would she listen to any advice from me, a stranger who had no right to comment on private matters—even if such were a part of murder?

I braced myself for a coming struggle. Then once more I heard voices from the very room which was my target. Another quarrel with Anne? The door was not firmly closed—

I rapped and the sound was followed by a dead silence. Then a voice—Maud's—

"Go away! Please go away!"

But her cry was overridden by Miss Austin's more precise voice: "Come in—at once!"

I chose to obey the second order, and opened the door. Miss Austin sat up in bed, a mound of pillows supporting her back. Save that the bed-clothes were pulled up and she wore a crocheted bed jacket, she was in as much command of the scene as she would have been fully clothed and sitting in her parlor chair.

"Come in," she ordered for the second time.

Maud stood defiantly between me and the bed, as if she would bar me if she quite dared. Outwardly the maid was her usual stiffly starched self. But in whatever battle had raged Miss Austin had triumphed. Maud might glower, and did, but she could not protest my intrusion.

"Perhaps *you* can tell me just what is going on in this house!" Miss Elizabeth frowned at Maud but addressed me. "When I ask a simple question, I expect a truthful and forthright answer." I decided that remark must have been aimed at Maud. "The police are here again, are they not?"

Since Miss Elizabeth's windows did not overlook the drive, I wondered how she had learned that—unless Maud had told her.

"Yes, Miss Austin." I confined myself to the simple truth she said she wanted.

"Why?"

This seemed to me an opening for my mission.

"That they would like to explain to you in person, Miss Austin."

"Sent you up to say that, did they? You needn't answer. Any simpleton could guess that. Well, they shall just wait until I am ready."

All the decisiveness she had shown at our first meeting was back. Miss Austin had the appearance of one well ready not only to defend her own position, but to carry war into the enemy camp.

"Now tell me the truth, Miss Jansen, why are they here? What have they found out about Roderick?"

I was forced into a half-truth. "They don't tell us anything—they just ask questions—"

"And you answer those questions, is that it? It never pays to let authority have matters all their own way, you know. And what kind of questions have they been asking? You never knew Roderick, did you? What would they have then to ask you? Nothing to answer seems to have taken quite a while—"

How did Miss Austin know how long I had been in the library? Was she just guessing, or was Maud eyes and ears for her mistress?

"Roderick Frimsbee was a sorry man and disgrace alive, and he will cause even more trouble now that he is dead," Miss Elizabeth observed dispassionately. "What new crime of his have they discovered?"

"None that I know of, Miss Austin." I was glad we were sticking to the comparatively safe ground of Roderick. Yet, should Miss Elizabeth decide to speak to the police, she should be warned that it was a second murder which had brought them here.

I might have guessed she would be too shrewd for

me—just as Aunt Otilda had always been. Now the old lady spoke again, slowly, as if pausing to gather strength after each word.

"Your face gives you away, my girl. This concerns more than just Roderick now. What do they want?"

I made one last effort; they should never have sent me to do this. But my conditioning by Aunt Otilda was too strong to resist. Miss Elizabeth had produced just the tone of voice to which I had been trained to answer.

"If you will just see them, Miss Austin—"

"When I am ready, not before," she flashed back. "Tell me, what are they after now?"

"It is about Mrs. Horvath." The silence became intense.

"Miss Emma!" Maud's voice was choked. "What about Miss Emma?" she demanded shrilly.

Against the pillow Miss Austin's back was ramrod straight, but there was a new look on her face, a coldness. I had heard of icy rages. Now I believed I was witnessing the results of one such.

"What about my sister?"

There was no withstanding her demand, no twists or turns I could use to evade the truth.

"They say she was poisoned."

I heard Maud cry out. But there was no alteration in Miss Austin's expression. It was as if she had anticipated just such a statement, had been steeling herself to meet it.

"Maud, ask Miss Irene to come here—at once!" Her tone held the crack of a whip, and I was not surprised to see Maud go out meekly. But I had not yet been dismissed.

"How?" she asked.

Again dissimulation was beyond me. "Something to do with a box of preserved ginger."

Miss Austin's hands were clasped before her. She stared past—*through*—me, as if I had ceased to exist. The ticking of the clock on the mantel was all which broke the quiet.

"What do you want, Aunt? Stuart is very sick. I can't leave him—" Irene came in.

"I want to talk to you," said Miss Elizabeth, and Irene seemed drawn forward from the door by the force of the older woman's will. "Maud will stay with Stuart. Yes, I mean that, Maud!"

For a moment it looked as if Maud, hovering in the doorway, might mutiny. Thankfully I followed her into the hall, but I was not to escape so easily.

"Please, miss." Maud caught at my sleeve. "Don't go yet. Miss Elizabeth, she ain't as well as she seems. It's her heart, but she won't admit it. Now she's all worked up, and it's bad for her. Please stay here, miss, and call me if she has one of her spells!" She ended on such an imploring note I could not deny her and nodded.

"—tell the truth!" The words delivered in Miss Austin's stern voice carried out into the hall.

"I have told the truth!" Anger and impatience colored Irene's reply.

"I cannot disbelieve the evidence of my own eyes, wretched girl. I saw you Wednesday night—do you understand? I was witness to your infamous conduct. And the time has come when I can no longer conceal that from the police. Emma—Emma was a forceful personality, she could be both callous and cruel. I have always been clear-sighted concerning my sister. But that is no excuse for murder. If fear drove you to that act on Wednesday night, that, too, I can understand. We are all creatures played upon by our emotions and we react differently. You have never impressed me, Irene, as a person of strong will or purpose. I must admit, therefore, your actions have surprised me. There is more in you than I ever expected to find. But I am now telling you the truth. After this moment I shall cease to keep silence on your behalf. Do you understand me?"

"You—you're mad!" Irene's voice shook. It held, I thought, a ragged note of fear. "I don't know what you're talking about. You must be mad!"

"Sunday you went with me to visit Emma," Miss Austin continued. "I even encouraged you to make the trip. Emma had not acted fairly towards you. I had some hopes that once she had had time to consider matters, she might change her mind. Emma was exceedingly fond of ginger. Even greedy where it was concerned."

"Yes, I took her some ginger. But what's all this about? Aunt, what are you trying to tell me?"

I put my hand to the doorknob. Surely this confrontation could be doing Miss Austin little good if Maud's warning about her heart was correct.

"The police are here. They say Emma was poisoned."

"*No!*" The single word was a scream. "No, I won't

believe it! You're wicked—just as cruel as she was. You're mad!"

I had just time to step back before Irene burst out of the room.

"She's mad—mad!" Her hands were at her mouth, her eyes wide with fear. She pushed past, running towards her own room.

"Hmmm—"

Startled I nearly jumped. Sergeant Blake's sturdy bulk loomed there. He must have come up the back stairs. How much had he overheard? He was going away and, once Blake reported, the lieutenant might come up himself. I went back to face Miss Elizabeth.

"The police sergeant was just outside. I think he overheard some of what you said to Irene. He's gone to report."

"Very well." Miss Austin retained her composure. If the scene with her nephew's wife had troubled her any, she did not show that. "Very well. Let him come if he wishes."

"Miss Austin, would you like me to call the doctor? He could forbid their questioning you—"

"There comes a time when truth must out. I have been very weak, influenced by matters which should not have made any difference. My nephew Roderick was a sly, greedy boy. He grew up to be an evil and devious man. Perhaps to shield the innocent—I would have—I have done things which are abhorrent to me. But Emma's death is another matter altogether. Emma was hard, but she was not evil. And she should not have died before her time."

I thought that last statement must be important to

anyone as old as Miss Austin—the thought of a sudden and murderous death. Death might stand by the door, but should not enter until the right time, not be summoned by violence.

"If it was true," she said, "if Emma was really poisoned—then—"

"Then what, Miss Austin?"

Lieutenant Daniels had entered the door I must have left open. Behind him was Mark.

"Come in." Miss Elizabeth chose to ignore the fact that Daniels was already a step or so inside. "You may be seated—there—"

When they were seated, just as she had indicated, she continued calmly:

"You informed Miss Jansen that my sister died unnaturally—of poison."

Daniels glared at me. I stared coolly back.

"Yes."

"This has been proven beyond a doubt?"

"Yes."

For a second or two Miss Austin closed her eyes.

"And my nephew Roderick?"

"He was shot, perhaps sometime Saturday night."

"He was also engaged in some criminal activity, or else was in hiding after the commission of such a crime?"

"What makes you ask that, Miss Austin?" Mark wanted to know.

"I have known Roderick ever since a short time after he was born. He was always a trouble and a source of family disgrace. The fact that he did not come openly to this house, but apparently remained in hiding on the grounds, conveys the supposition that he was in difficulties of one kind or another."

"You have little sympathy with your nephew then?" Daniels wanted to know.

"It was impossible for me to have any sympathy for Roderick. His was a twisted nature, and, from early boyhood, he caused only sorrow and disappointment. By my father's orders, he was exiled from the family. I have heard nothing of or from him for years."

"Then you have no idea of who may have wanted him dead?"

"What is your name, please?" She looked directly at Mark when he asked that question.

Hurriedly I introduced him.

"Are you also of the police, Colonel Rohmer?"

"No, Miss Austin. I am in government service."

"But you are here because of Roderick. He was engaged in some sort of crime against his country, is that what you must tell me?"

"We are not sure, Miss Austin. I am really only investigating rumors."

"Which, knowing Roderick, I am prepared to accept as true." Again her eyes closed for a long moment. "But I assure you that I know absolutely nothing of my nephew and his concerns. I did not even know he was in this country until—until—" Her voice trailed away.

"Miss Austin." Daniels spoke then. "It is not primarily your nephew's death we have come to see you about—now—"

"Emma—" Her lips visibly shaped the word without speaking it aloud.

"Yes, Mrs. Horvath. You knew that her body, taken

from the coffin, had been lightly buried in the grave opened in your private plot?"

The assenting inclination of her head was slight.

"In fact, Miss Austin, you were aware of the substitution of your nephew's body for that of Mrs. Horvath before the coffin was opened, is that not so?"

"I was." Her voice was firmer than I expected to hear. "That is, I was aware of an exchange of bodies. I was not aware that the man was Roderick."

"Suppose," Mark said quietly, "you tell us about it, Miss Austin."

"I was unable to sleep," she began. "Though Emma and I had never been close, we were sisters after all, and her sudden and unexpected death—when she seemed to be so much better—came as a shock. I found myself dreading the funeral, and was unable to compose myself. It is my custom when I am so disturbed to brew a cup of a herb tea of my own blending—I have found such most efficacious to quiet mind and nerves."

A herb blend? Miss Austin, then, had still room for knowledge of brewing and blending?

"I made my tea and drank it and was about to return to my room when I heard a noise in the hall leading to the garden door. Since the hour was late and I knew all the members of the household were supposedly in their beds, I decided it well to investigate. What I saw—" she paused, not looking at any of us but at the wall as if she viewed there the scene she described—"was so astounding that for a few moments I was under the impression I was in the grip of a nightmare.

"A man and a woman were going toward the front of the house, supporting between them a third person. From the limpness of his body I was inclined to believe he was either unconscious or dead."

"And who were this man and woman?" Daniels asked as Miss Elizabeth fell silent and was touching her lips with a fine handkerchief.

"It was dark, and I was so surprised and, I will admit, frightened, that I did not endeavor to see their faces. They went on into the parlor. I was so unstrung—I have a heart condition which I do not pamper but which limits me at times—that I had to sit down on the steps of the back staircase trying to get my breath. I may even have lost consciousness for a short period. I do know that when I was again aware of my surrounding I saw the man coming back, another burden in his arms." Her eyes were closed, her face gray.

Mark spoke swiftly. "You need not tell us about that, Miss Austin. We can guess what you saw."

Again she touched the handkerchief to her lips. "Thank you. After the man was gone, I managed to reach the parlor door. It was my intention to see what was going on before I called the police."

"And why didn't you—call the police, I mean?" asked Daniels.

"Because I saw a member of my own family closing the coffin. The scandal—in the past we have had two scandals—one of which ruined my father's life. And this member—well, there were good reasons for me to consider other factors before I called in the authorities. I still had not adjusted to what I had witnessed. I could not at that moment face a scene with the person involved. The man might return at any moment, and his actions had led me to believe that he was a ruthless person. I withdrew into the library and allowed my relative to leave the parlor unaware of my presence. Later I locked the garden door. If the man did return he was unable to enter the house.

"Miss Jansen found me quite overcome in the upper hall and took me to my room. My physical condition then clouded my mind for a space. I felt that I simply could not face a public revelation of what had happened. Though I might have known such a deed could not go undiscovered. Now you tell me that Emma was also murdered—"

"And who was this relative you saw, whom you have been shielding, Miss Austin?" Daniels went straight to the heart of the matter.

"My nephew's wife, Irene."

"And the man?" questioned Mark.

She shook her head. "He—that was what made me believe I could not trust my eyes—he had one of those ski masks over his head!"

"But Irene was not disguised?" Mark asked.

"No."

11

If Miss Austin had surprised Daniels, he showed no sign of it.

"What contact did Mrs. Irene Frimsbee have with her brother-in-law?"

"None that I was aware of. That's why—I can't really understand. As far as I know they never met. Roderick had cut almost all ties with the family before Charles married Irene. Why she should now—" A faint shudder shook her thin body. "The why of that scene, to which I was a most unwilling witness, you will have to discover from Irene herself. Charles' health has been a great worry to her, and her little boy is very delicate. To my knowledge, that is all which has truly occupied her mind for a long time."

"And Mrs. Horvath ordered her out of the house she thought was hers only a short time ago." Daniels made that a statement rather than a question. "Wasn't Mrs. Frimsbee very much upset over that?"

"Yes, as was only natural. It was her understanding, one which I must state was shared by all of us, that the carriage house had been an outright gift to her husband upon their marriage. She had spent a lot of time and effort bringing it to its present state as a comfortable home. To be deprived of it so arbitrarily came as a shock."

"Why did Mrs. Horvath do that?" Mark's lower voice was in contrast to Daniel's official tone.

"During the past half year my sister has—did—make a number of decisions which appeared strange. It is my belief she was engaged in some private enterprise which she did not wish revealed to the family. She displayed a sudden and unusual desire to assess ready cash and argued that she needed the rent which the Cantrells were willing to pay for the carriage house. In addition she told Irene, most tactlessly, that since Charles' complete recovery was only problematical and they now had a child—which she deplored, under the circumstances—it was best another arrangement be made as soon as possible." Miss Elizabeth spoke with the dispassionate summing up of a judge. "I must also, in fairness, add that my sister had a hasty tongue. She very often said, during the heat of momentary annoyance, things which she did not mean later. However, one's words, rather than the emotions from which they spring, are all the hearer has to base a judgment upon."

"And Mrs. Frimsbee based hers so? She had good reason to hate her husband's aunt?"

Mark cut in with another question before she could answer. "You say that it was lately that Mrs. Horvath indicated she needed money for some purpose?"

"That is correct. Emma had the income of a trust. Of course, as we all know, such fixed incomes do not stand up well in this time of continued inflation. Alexis Horvath also held the reactionary belief that women had no place in business. Ever since her marriage, Emma had to be secretive about her money. I believe she had holdings of her own, built up over the years by shrewd investments. But to all outward appearances she lived on the trust income and prided herself on spending every penny of that by the end of the year."

"And if she needed quite a sum of money—" Daniels got to the point. "And didn't want to admit she had a nest egg stashed away, she'd have to cut down a lot in public and let everyone know about it?"

"Exactly. Such a situation would appeal to Emma. She knew that the trust income, after her death, would go to Hanno. But I am confident that her personal estate is larger than she allowed anyone to guess. Emma was a devious person. She would display an intense interest in one object, while secretly she was engaged in procuring another. She also had our father's talent for concentration—only she applied that in other fields than scholarship."

In ways you did not approve, I translated to myself.

"You say my sister was poisoned—with ginger?"

Daniels' expression expressed surprise. "I don't think ginger was mentioned."

Miss Elizabeth made an impatient gesture. "Young

man, let us not quibble. I assure you that you shall find me far more cooperative if you tell me the truth and not try to lay traps. Now answer this. Was Emma truly poisoned and was the poison conveyed to her in a box of preserved ginger?"

For a second or two the lieutenant hesitated. He did not look in my direction but I could guess that he blamed me for this. However, it was plain that in Miss Elizabeth he had met his match.

"Yes, to both questions."

"And the nature of the poison?"

His hesitation was of longer duration this time. But at last he replied:

"The pathologist called it 'staphisagriae semina.' It comes from—"

"The ripe seeds of the delphinium." Her hands were pressed tightly together.

"You have delphiniums in the garden here."

"That is no secret. The Abbey delphiniums in the past years have been most noteworthy." But her reply sounded absent. She seemed to be thinking of something else.

"Sergeant!" Blake materialized in the doorway. "Ask Mrs. Irene Frimsbee to come here."

We waited in silence. Miss Elizabeth's eyes were closed. As if, her stern duty done, she withdrew from what might follow. There was the sound of protesting voices in the hall, and then, flushed, her hair straggling, her mouth set stubbornly, Irene Frimsbee came in.

She broke away from that light touch on her arm which the sergeant had exerted, and went to the foot of the bed, where she stood glaring in undisguised anger at Miss Austin, who took no notice of her.

"What did you tell them?" she cried. "You're mad—absolutely mad! You should have been put away long ago with that old witch of a sister! Cracked old hags, both of you! She trying to stay young, running around with men young enough to be her sons. And you—clinging to this house, pretending your father was a scholar, when he was nothing but a queer old dead-beat living off his relations in order to buy books. You're all mad—" Her voice broke and she began to cry, making no move to wipe the tears from her face.

"Cut it out, lady!" Sergeant Blake said as if his sense of propriety had been offended.

Miss Elizabeth might not have heard a word. Daniels, I believed, was well content to let Irene continue. But at the sergeant's words, her mouth closed, she looked around as if sudden realization dampened her rage.

"You accompanied Miss Austin to visit Mrs. Horvath last Sunday?" Daniels began in a formal tone of voice.

Irene only nodded.

"And you took your aunt a small gift? A tin of preserved ginger?"

"She wasn't *my* aunt. Neither of them is." Her gaze swung from Daniels to Miss Austin, as if daring the older woman to contradict her.

"Your husband's aunt," Daniels amended. "But you did take her a tin of ginger?"

"She liked ginger." Irene neither affirmed nor denied his question.

"Where did you buy this ginger?"

"I didn't buy it. Someone sent it to Charles." Her voice was dull, her shoulders sagged. She had a beaten look, as if Miss Elizabeth's failure to answer her tirade had pulled away her prop of righteous anger. "He doesn't like it. When I went out to see him, he gave it to me and said to pass it on to Aunt Emma."

"It was in a metal container." That was Mark. "Was the container sealed in any way?"

She frowned. "I—I think so. There was a band of red tape where the lid opened. Charles hadn't opened it. He doesn't like it."

"So you brought it from the hospital here." Daniels went on. "What did you do with it then?"

"I don't remember. It must have been in my room—no," she corrected that. "I left it on the table in the downstairs hall, the one where we leave mail. I thought if I put it away I might forget about it. Keeping it in sight would remind me."

"This table in the hall." The Lieutenant turned to Miss Austin. "Just where is it?"

She opened her eyes. Her gaze was impersonal, detached, as if all of us and the problems we represented no longer meant much to her.

"It is a small marble-topped table just by the door to the parlor. It is customary to spread out the mail there so that guests may take their own letters at their convenience. Small parcels are also left there. Irene's leaving her package there would be perfectly natural."

Perhaps her words did reassure Irene. For her head came up and she faced the lieutenant squarely.

"I left it right there. That was Friday night. As far as I know it remained there until I picked it up on Sunday."

Daniels plainly did not care for the implications in that. But it was Mark who asked:

"Did you examine it when you picked it up Sunday?"

"Examine it? No, why should I? I twisted a piece of paper around it. We were in a hurry. There was a taxi waiting. But what's this all about—what was wrong with the ginger?"

Now it was Miss Elizabeth who spoiled any plan the lieutenant may have had. "The ginger was poisoned—with delphinium seeds."

"Oh no!" Irene's hand went to her mouth, she shrank back as if physically threatened.

Then Daniels attacked. "Why did you substitute the body of Roderick Frimsbee for that of Mrs. Horvath in the coffin? Who helped you do that?"

Her mouth was agape. She eyed the lieutenant as if he had gone raving mad before her eyes. Her astonishment became fear.

"I—did—*what?*"

"We have a witness to the fact that you helped substitute one body for the other," Daniels continued relentlessly. "Why was Roderick killed and by whom?"

I saw Irene sway, as Mark must have seen also. For by the time I reached the girl, he was with me and had caught her as she slumped forward over the foot of the bed.

We got Irene to the chaise longue and she began to

moan, but her eyes remained closed. And I was convinced she would not admit recovery. Daniels rammed his fists into his coat pockets.

"Fantastic," he muttered. "The whole thing is fantastic!"

"No, sir, you can't go in." We heard the sergeant. Daniels strode over and opened the door.

"What's the matter?"

"I demand to know, sir, by what right you have intruded on Miss Austin? Just what are all of you doing in her room? She is ill. This treatment will certainly not be countenanced by your superiors. They shall hear of your high-handed action!"

"Preston!" Miss Elizabeth did not raise her voice, but it brought an end to his protest. Mr. Donner elbowed his way past the police.

"There is no need for a display of knight-errantry, Preston," she said in a quelling way. "I have thought it wise to tell all I knew. It is now proved that Emma was poisoned, murdered as was Roderick. We must help and not hinder the police."

"You have considered this carefully, Miss Elizabeth?"

"I have, Preston. You know that I believe Roderick's death came out of his way of life. But Emma's is different. I desire to see her murderer caught."

"Very well, Miss Elizabeth, if that is what you wish—"

"Yes, that's right! You're her tame cat, ready to back up what insane lie she tells!" Irene came abruptly to life, pulling herself up on the lounge, her eyes blazing. "Go ahead, help her tell the police how I poisoned Aunt Emma—how I got up at night and dragged her body out of the coffin. And all the rest of the mad story she's dreamed up! What good would all that do me? What would I get out of murdering Aunt Emma—tell *me* that! Who gets her money now?" She pointed to Miss Elizabeth. "She does! Didn't Aunt Emma tell us so when she said she was going to make that new will? As for Roderick—I'd never seen him before, except in a photograph until Mother Frimsbee had the coffin opened. And that's the truth!"

Across that frantic declaration Miss Austin's voice cut like an avenging sword. "Emma was poisoned with delphinium seeds—"

Irene cowered back as if those words were blows. Preston Donner started.

"Delphinium—" Then his mouth closed firmly.

"Suppose," Daniels said, his voice was close to a purr, "you explain about the delphinium seeds, Miss Austin. Each mention of them apparently is upsetting to you all."

Miss Elizabeth, in her role of avenging fate, did have an answer.

"My sister was not interested in gardening. But the fame of our delphinium beds is widespread. She promised seeds to some friends of hers two years ago. She took to harvest the seeds herself, most unfortunately as it turned out. At the time there was a small abrasion on her hand, and that was irritated to a serious infection. The doctor warned her that she was highly allergic to the plant. She was seriously ill for several days."

"And all of you," Daniels said, including Donner and Irene, "knew about this?"

Irene made no reply. The look of fright on her face answered for her. Preston Donner gave a curt nod.

"Who else knew about it?"

"All those who were living here at the time," Miss Austin replied. "Including my sister Anne and Hanno——"

"Miss Lowndes was not a resident here then?" Mark wanted to know.

"No."

"But," Daniels observed, "she could have heard of Mrs. Horvath's allergy from any one of you."

"A stranger—why should she—" Miss Austin began.

"No." The fire had gone of Irene, she spoke in a dull, beaten voice. "You prefer to lie about me. Why? What have I ever done to you?"

She got up, her hand on the bedpost for support.

"I have always tried to be honest." She might have been talking to herself rather than attempting to justify her actions to us. "I couldn't pretend to grieve for Aunt Emma. She was dirt-mean to us. Sometimes I think she enjoyed seeing how miserable she could make people. But I didn't kill her, and I didn't have anything to do with the switching of the bodies."

"Miss Austin, are you willing to swear that the woman you saw that night was Mrs. Frimsbee?" asked Mark slowly.

Miss Elizabeth's reply was firmly final. "I will swear to that in court—if such a distasteful action becomes necessary."

"How you must hate me," Irene said in a drained voice, "and I don't even know why."

"The tin of ginger was left on a table in the hallway from Friday night to Sunday morning," Mark observed. "Mr. Donner, we understand that table is also used for mail, and those who live here visit it to pick up their letters. Did you have any on Saturday?"

"Mail—Saturday? Why yes, I received the catalog of the Lewiston sale. It must have come Saturday because I at once wired in a bid on the Trancati folder. That I can be sure of."

"Do you remember any other mail or small packages on the table when you picked up your catalog?"

"I came home at half-past three." Preston began to reconstruct his afternoon in his usual hesitating and precise voice. "I went right over to look at the mail. Mine mainly consisted of business communications. There were four or five letters, several magazines, my catalog. But packages—" he closed his eyes as if so to better visualize the table. "No, I don't remember any packages at all."

"Not conclusive," Daniels commented to Mark.

"Yes, but a start."

"Mrs. Frimsbee." Daniels was back to Irene. "There are some more questions."

Irene drew away from the bedpost, which had been her support.

"Stuart's sick, one of his bad colds. Do you mind if go to look in on him now?"

"The sergeant will go with you."

But before she was out of the room Preston Donner

cried out and sprang to the side of the bed. Miss Austin, her iron will giving way at last, had slumped among her pillows. For one horrified instant I thought she was dead.

Confusion followed. The doctor was summoned, Maud called. When they were in charge of the sickroom, Mark drew me aside.

"Stick to Irene," he ordered.

"You think she might try to run away? But I'm sure she won't leave her child."

"No, I'm sure of that. So you think she's guilty?"

I was not sure. Irene's attitude had impressed me. I did not believe she was enough of an actress to put on such a show of bewildered innocence. On the other hand, Miss Elizabeth's testimony—

"If Miss Elizabeth just didn't seem so sure—"

"Yes, but even an honest witness can be wrong. Only, stick with Irene."

Though I did not want to, I found myself promising that I would do so. I went to knock on her door as Mark disappeared down the stairs. Sergeant Blake opened, and there was a shade of relief on his face.

"Glad you are here, miss. The lieutenant said it is okay." He stepped by me and was gone.

Irritated I rapped for the second time. What I could do, I had no idea, and if I wasn't asked in—did Mark expect me to play sentry in the hall?

Irene opened the door this time. With no expression on her face she stepped back to let me enter.

"I suppose you're to watch me. I'd never have taken you for a policewoman."

"I'm not. I came to see if I could be of help."

She shrugged. "Have it your own way. I'm not running away. I told the truth—Stuart is really sick. Come and see for yourself." Her fingers closed in a vise grip about my wrist as she tugged me across the disorderly bedroom to a small alcove. Three-quarters of the space was occupied by a crib.

In a huddle of blankets lay a little boy, squirming restlessly, his face flushed, his hair in rough peaks. One arm lay across a panda bear, and he was breathing in gasps. Though I had had small experience with children, I could see he was ill enough to worry over.

Beside him Irene lost her fumbling awkwardness. She was sure, alert, efficient, as she adjusted a vaporizer to send a cloud of aromatic steam across the crib.

"All these colds! I wish we could get away from here, go where it is warm. It isn't fair!" She stood over the vaporizer, solicitude and weariness at war on her haggard face. "If we only had a fraction of Aunt Emma's income we could go South. But—" She rounded on me. "None of it comes to us—not one red cent! They can't say that it does. She told Charles three months ago, before her accident, that she was cutting him out of her will." Irene bent over the restless child, touching his face with a gentle finger, putting both panda and arm back under the covers.

"Is Dr. Bains still here?" she asked.

"I think so."

"He must take another look at Stuart. But I'm not going to send him to the hospital. Stuart would be frightened to death. Oh!" Her fist hammered on the crib rail. "I wish I knew what to do! What can I do?"

Before I could move, she sped to the door and was out and gone. By the time I followed she was up the hall, hammering on Miss Austin's door.

A chill draft swept around my ankles. Remembering the child, I closed the door. Very much at a loss, I went back to the crib. The steam continued, and I thought he seemed to be breathing easier. His head turned as he uttered a little sighing moan.

Surely Irene should be back with the doctor. I looked at the door, just in time to see a bit of paper slipped under it. Once more I crossed the room, but when I opened the door the hallway was empty. I stooped and picked up the note.

The paper was smooth-edged on three sides, the fourth raggedly torn. It might have been the end page of a book. Across it, in a pointed script I had never seen before, were two lines.

"Keep your mouth shut. Or you and Stuart will be sorry."

The name Stuart had been underlined so sharply there was a tiny hole in the paper.

A genuine threat? Or could Irene have planted it herself to lift suspicion? At any rate, Mark was going to see this. If the younger Mrs. Frimsbee had planted it, my silence now might lead her to a false and betraying move. If she had not—why add to her worries? I tucked the note into my jacket pocket just as she came in.

"Dr. Bains will be here in a minute—"

"Did you see anyone in the hall a few minutes ago?" She shook her head impatiently. "I wasn't in the

hall. I went into Aunt's room. No, I didn't see anyone."

But Irene had been in the hall herself, I thought. So
very easy for her to plant the note. I must show it to
Mark as soon as I could.

12

I thought that Stuart Frimsbee was seriously ill, so I was surprised to hear the doctor reassure Irene that by tomorrow the boy should show definite signs of improvement. But he had other news also.

"I wish that all was as well with Miss Austin."

"Is she very ill?" I asked.

He glanced at me. "Ill? We are waiting now for the ambulance. The sooner we get her to the hospital and under oxygen, the better."

"Then there is something wrong with her heart after all," Irene commented.

The doctor frowned. "Miss Austin is one of those individuals, unfortunately only too common in her generation, who will not seek any medical help until it is almost too late. As far as I can determine, she must have experienced warning symptons for some time. But did she see me or any other physician? No, she dosed herself with herbal remedies of her own concoction. It's a wonder she didn't poison herself."

Those last four words hung in the air, and he must have realized at once how unfortunate under the circumstances his complaint had been, for after giving a few instructions, he left.

Irene pulled the blankets straight over her son. There was a brooding expression on her face that suggested she was not thinking of Stuart. The hasty comment of the doctor lingered in my own mind. Could it be a key to the puzzle? If the answer was yes, it only proved again what a bad judge of character I was.

To conceive of Miss Austin committing murder and covering her act with bald accusations of Irene was, to me, sheer insanity. Though motive, knowledge, and opportunity had all been hers.

The shriek of an ambulance siren could be heard even through the Abbey walls. Going to the door, I witnessed Miss Elizabeth's departure, accompanied by the doctor, a nurse, and Maud. Preston Donner brought up the rear, his face now as nearly gray in tint as his coat.

"She's gone." Irene spoke for the first time since the doctor left. "I wish—I wish she had told the truth!"

My fingers closed over the note in my pocket. Now was the time to locate Mark and hand that over. Irene had drawn a chair close to the crib and settled in it.

"I'll be back," I told her. I did not know whether that was a promise or a warning.

Anne Frimsbee had not appeared, neither had

Leslie. If they knew of Miss Austin's departure, they had not chosen to witness it.

I hurried down the stairs. There was no one in the wide lower hall. The silence was thick, as if this was now a deserted house. I was startled as one of the detectives appeared.

"You are looking for someone, miss?"

"Colonel Rohmer."

"Sorry, he left about twenty minutes ago."

"Do you know where I can reach him?"

"You can try headquarters." He gave me a number, which I kept repeating as I went on to the back hall and the phone.

I dialed, and to an answering masculine growl, I repeated my request for Mark, to be disappointed a second time. Should I now ask for Lieutenant Daniels? Leslie, coming into view, made me change my mind.

Even her polished surface had been scratched by the events of the past hours. Lines showed on her face. Instead of a timeless thirty, she could now be thought a care-ridden forty.

"Do you know what time it is?" she demanded. "Twenty to eight. I've called the market and they've agreed to deliver—for an extra fee. Reena's just walked out. She's locked in her room and won't talk to anyone. If we're going to have anything to eat tonight, we'll get it ourselves. And—" She leaned against the wall. "I'm beat. Another day like this one, and I'll take to my bed also."

"They've taken Miss Austin to the hospital."

"I saw her go. With Preston and Hanno tagging in

Hanno's car. We needn't expect them back soon. Irene with Stuart?"

Perhaps I was overwrought, ready to read meanings where they were not intended. But I sensed contempt in the intonation of that last question. Almost as if Leslie was rather cynically amused at Irene's preoccupation with her child. I must try not to imagine things.

"You say you ordered groceries?"

"Yes. We're lucky the market was still open. Goodness knows, I'm not the world's best cook, but I can boil an egg. You willing to lend a hand? There—" She was interrupted by the sound of a bell. "That must be the delivery now. Come and see what we were able to get."

I helped Leslie check the bags and boxes. And I noted my companion paid strict attention to prices, totaling up the bill expertly. Money, I suspected, was one of the subjects Leslie did not find amusing.

"I'll go up and see what Irene wants," I offered as Leslie lined up the purchases on the table.

"All right," she replied absently, reading the directions on a box of biscuit mix.

In spite of the light now on in the hall gloom seeped up through the house. It was chilly, too. I shivered, wondering if any check had been made lately on the furnace. Perhaps I had better ask Leslie about that.

Irene was not alone. Seated on the chair pulled close to the crib was Anne. She was talking in a low voice, but as I entered the half-open door, their heads jerked apart.

"What is it, Miss Jansen?" Anne's veneer of friendliness had cracked.

I found myself using an apologetic tone which I immediately resented.

"Miss Lowndes has had some groceries delivered and is going to prepare supper. Do you need anything special for Stuart?"

"I would be grateful for a cup of warm milk," Irene returned. "Mother Frimsbee, you should at leave have a cup of tea—"

But Anne was not about to agree.

"No, my dear. I had quite a substantial tea with Miss Jansen earlier." Subtly she so accused me of being heartlessly occupied with food, when finer souls, such as herself, arose above the material. "My nerves are in such a jangle now I could not eat a bite. This is too exhausting. All those questions from the police— simply stupid, most of them. But Irene, my dear, Stuart is sleeping. Why don't you run down while he is resting well and have something yourself? You can't go without food. I shall stay right here until you return."

Perhaps Irene might have accepted that offer, though her reconciliation with Anne surprised me. But there came a rap on the door and Sergeant Blake looked in.

"Mrs. Irene Frimsbee—I would like to speak to you—"

As Irene stood up, the sergeant continued. "The lieutenant wants to see you downtown right away."

Irene stiffened. But she had gained control after her confrontation with Miss Elizabeth.

"I have a small child who is sick. I cannot leave him."

"The lieutenant talked to Dr. Bains. He's sending over a nurse to stay with the boy."

"Irene, my dear," Anne said, "I'll stay with Stuart. And the sooner you settle this nonsense, the better. Elizabeth was, of course, completely irrational when she made those absurd statements. You can easily prove that once you discuss things with the lieutenant. Remember that the important thing is that all this must be kept from Charles."

Irene nodded. Her face was blank as she pulled the plaid coat out of the closet and put it on, tied a scarf over her head. Her actions showed the determination of one committed to a course of action.

"Let's go," she said. "The sooner we get there, the sooner I'll be back."

She said no goodbyes but marched out a step or two ahead of her escort. Anne remained by the door, seeming to listen, until the sound of a slam reached us. Then she favored me with one of those stretches of lips she apparently considered a smile.

"The warm milk for Stuart, Miss Jansen—do you suppose you could bring that up later? There is a pill he is supposed to take with it in about forty minutes."

"Yes." I was still surprised at Irene's abrupt departure. She must have gained new support from some quarter. I paused by the phone on my way to the kitchen, for the second time, only to hang up before an answer when I heard the faint creak of a door above. I had no intention of speaking about the note if Anne could hear me.

The kitchen was a haven of warmth after the

growing chill of the halls, and Leslie was busy. She slid a pan of biscuits into the oven as I entered.

"What now?"

"The police have asked Irene to go downtown. Dr. Bains's nurse is coming to look after Stuart."

She closed the oven door. "So they want to question Irene again? But why, in the name of heaven? That poor creature couldn't have gotten up nerve enough to dispose of Miss Emma—let alone arrange that very unfunny coffin joke. She's a mouse all through—even the police ought to see that."

"Miss Austin seems to think she had done both." I wanted to see Leslie's reaction. After all, she knew Miss Elizabeth much better than I, and whether Miss Austin was indeed capable of lying so convincingly.

"Miss Elizabeth Austin lives with the conviction that she is always right, but it is amazing how many times in the past she has been wrong. If the police have picked Irene for their number-one suspect, I have lost all confidence in their collective intelligence."

"Who do you think is guilty?"

Leslie used the can opener on a jam-pot lid. "Our Roderick was a black sheep and must have picked up any number of enemies during his career. As for Emma Horvath, well, there Miss Elizabeth herself had an excellent motive. This ghastly house is a white elephant. She can't sell it by the terms of her father's will, and the taxes are going up every year. There's very little money to keep it up. You don't think she makes enough out of us, her 'guests,' to cover expenses, do you? But she does get a good slice of Emma's own private holdings, and with that she doesn't have to worry.

She must have reached a time in life when she is tired of worrying. No, Miss Elizabeth could well have hurried Emma along. She knew plants and herbs. Then that switch in bodies spoiled her game by making the police suspicious of Emma's death. I'll wager she could willingly have added Anne to her bag for exposing it."

"But Roderick—who *would* switch bodies? Miss Austin simply could not have done that."

"I agree. In addition to the physical impossibility, that bit is out of character for her. Consider this, however: suppose Roderick's death had nothing to do with the family at all. But the murderer saw a good chance—because of the private funeral—to cover his tracks. Two murders, but two different murderers. Then all the plans spoiled by Anne Frimsbee. It's perfectly possible. Do you like cheese?" She was slicing an orange-yellow wedge.

"If it's the sharp kind. But I wonder about your solution. A little improbable—"

"Oh, improbable things do happen now and then. You knew Colonel Rohmer before he turned up here, didn't you?"

I had been expecting that question for what now seemed days and I was prepared.

"I knew him slightly, years ago. But I had not seen him since—until I came here."

Leslie opened the oven to look at the biscuits. "He's very attractive." There was an interrogative note in her comment. I chose to ignore it. "But he's not police. He's in a hush-hush department, Gordon said. So it's my guess Roderick was mixed up in something important. He must have been to bring Rohmer into this."

"And that bolsters your theory?"

"Doesn't it? Do you see anyone in this house who might otherwise draw such attention?"

"I have an over-vivid imagination, but I have learned to distrust it. Your theory is too much like a story plot."

Leslie laughed. "I forgot that you and Theodosia are in the same trade. You are critical of my plotting sense?"

"It has always been my experience that the more fantastic and complicated the plot, the less well it works out. However, I make no guesses—"

"You don't have to. The plain facts are unbelievable enough. Though I will believe Irene Frimsbee is responsible only if she confesses it publicly."

The tinkle of a bell drew our attention to the old servants' call board on the wall. Leslie wiped her hands on her apron, the first out-of-character act I had ever seen her perform.

"Front door."

"Prbably the nurse."

"I'll let her in. Watch those biscuits, will you?"

She was gone. I set a pan of milk over a very low flame and checked the biscuits again. Then I warmed a cup in hot water and dried it, ready for the milk. Except for the sound of water bubbling in a pan of vegetables, and the loud ticking of a clock, the kitchen was very quiet.

I poured the milk into the cup and took another peek at the biscuits. Leslie must have escorted the nurse upstairs. It seemed as if she had been gone an unusually long time. If I waited any longer, I would have to reheat the milk. I took the precaution of turning off the oven, and started up the back stairs.

There was no sound in the house. I might have been the only person under that roof. The eerie feeling of loneliness persisted as I climbed the stairs. Before I reached the upper hall the phone began to ring with a shrill demand. Setting down the cup, I hurried back to answer.

"Is Miss Jansen there?"

Mark! I felt a warmth of relief as I answered. "I have been trying to get you."

"What happened?"

I no longer worried about an eavesdropper. Suddenly it was imperative to tell him about the note and I did so in as few words as possible.

"Then the lieutenant sent for Irene," I concluded.

"Yes, I know." Mark sounded tired. "Who's with the child now?"

"Anne Frimsbee. And the nurse Dr. Bains sent has just arrived, I believe."

"I'll be out as soon as it is humanly possible." A click. He had rung off.

Now the milk would have to be reheated. The kitchen was still deserted, and I was just in time to rescue a pan of cauliflower on the verge of boiling dry. Where was Leslie?

On impulse I went to the front of the house, peering into each dark room I passed. The breakfast room, that large dining room, the library, and lastly, and unwillingly, the parlor. No sign of Leslie.

When I returned to the kitchen, my feeling of being alone in the house grew menacing. It was all I could do to keep from running upstairs and pounding on bedroom doors. But I rewarmed the milk before I made the climb. With the cup in hand I stepped inside the still-ajar door of Irene's room.

"Here's—" My voice trailed into silence.

The chair, still pulled close to the crib, was empty. And the cot had been stripped bare. Both Stuart and his blankets were gone!

Anne must have taken the baby to her room for some reason, I told myself. I ran down the hall, and this time I did hammer on a door.

"Mrs. Frimsbee! Mrs. Frimsbee!"

There was the click of a turned key and her petulant voice reached me.

"What in the world is the matter?"

A weird figure faced me. Anne Frimsbee had prepared for bed. Her hair was in rollers, and her face shone with cream.

"What is the matter?" She repeated.

"Is Stuart with you? I brought up his milk, and I found the room empty. And where is the nurse?"

"Stuart?" Her expression was one of bewilderment. "But I don't understand you at all, Miss Jansen. Stuart is right where he should be, in his own crib. And the nurse is there with him—"

"But he isn't!" The fear I had been fighting ever since I had seen that empty crib closed in. "He isn't, I tell you! There's no one in the room at all!"

Anne Frimsbee pushed past me and ran, I followed. Her choked scream sounded as I joined her.

"You did leave them here?" I caught her by the

shoulder, gave her a slight shake. "The nurse was with Stuart?"

Her hands were locked about the rail of the crib, she stared down into that as if she could not believe what she saw. Or rather what she did not see.

"You left them here—" I repeated, "how long ago?"

Ann neither moved nor answered. I gave her a harder shake.

"Did you really leave them here—the baby and the nurse? When?"

Her trance was broken at last. "The baby—Leslie—"

I pulled her away from the crib and pushed her into the slipper chair.

"Now," I was forcing myself to speak calmly and slowly, "tell me exactly what happened."

Anne looked around the room as if searching for what she could not now see.

"I was here, sitting right here. And Stuart was asleep. He was breathing so much better—no more of that dreadfully sniffling. Then Leslie came in. She said that the nurse was here—the nurse Dr. Bains sent. She was in Leslie's room changing into her uniform. Leslie asked if I did not want to rest. She said she would bring me up a tray later. I was so tired, and Leslie said she would stay right here until the nurse came. So I went—I thought it was all right. Maybe—" A note of hope came into her voice. "Maybe the nurse took Stuart to the hospital. Dr. Bains wanted Irene to send him there, he spoke of it to me—"

"But she wouldn't do such a thing without your

knowledge or consent," I pointed out. "So you left Stuart with Leslie?"

"Yes. But why would the nurse take him away? And surely Leslie wouldn't—she had no reason to. Why, Leslie does not even like children. And she knew it would frighten me—"

"Frighten you!" The note! There was one person who might try to use Stuart to intimidate others, who was reckless enough for such a bold move. That was the unknown behind everything which had happened here. Leslie Lowndes?

"You never saw the nurse then?"

"No—but Leslie said— I can't see why she would—"

The door bell *had* rung. Whom had Leslie admitted, and why?

"Maybe Irene came back—" I heard Anne say.

Only half-heard, for I was already on my way to Leslie's room. The door of that was locked and my rapping brought no answer. I dropped to my knees and tried to see through the keyhole—only darkness. Then I went to search the other rooms. Miss Elizabeth's was disordered and empty. Anne Frimsbee's the same. The neat quarters of Preston Donner next. Hanno Horvath had also locked his door. Finally I returned to Anne.

"We must search the whole house."

There did remain the faint hope that Stuart had only been removed to some other room and not taken away. I passed a window and looked out into the night. I heard the soft hiss of snow against the pane. The ground below was already receiving a second white covering.

"But why?" Anne clawed at my arm. "Where is Leslie?"

"That is what we must find out." I shivered, thinking of that cold and snow without.

13

Still hoping against what I was afraid was a vain hope, I rounded on Anne briskly.

"Come on!"

But Mrs. Frimsbee, her robe hunched around her, her greasy face mirroring both bewilderment and fear, made no move.

"Where?"

"We must search the house. You know all the rooms. I don't," I retorted. "It's snowing again, a bad night. Who would take Stuart out in such weather?"

Her face crumpled. "The baby has such a bad cold. The nurse wouldn't take him—"

I dug my fingers into the plump shoulder beneath the covering of padded silk and propelled her by main force toward the door.

"I am beginning to believe there was never any nurse here."

That was too much for my captive. Anne stopped short, stiff and stubborn in my hold.

"Leslie said—I heard—" She began to babble.

"Please." I curbed my exasperation as best I could. "Come on, Mrs. Frimsbee, we must find Stuart and get him back to bed before he takes a fresh cold." But, I added to myself, will we find him at all?

Somehow I got Anne into the hall. There she stood while I made a fruitless second round of the unlocked rooms.

"What's on the third floor?" I pointed to the narrow flight of steps, an extension of the back stairs leading on upwards.

"Maud's room and Reena's, and the old ballroom. Elizabeth used that for storage."

"Where's the light switch?"

Anne pulled the full skirt of her robe about her, clutching it in one hand as she groped for the button. Then she did stumble her way up. At the head of the stairs, she pointed to one of the doors.

"That's the ballroom. Elizabeth keeps it locked, and I don't know where the key is."

I tried the door, confirmed it was locked. One of the two other doors yielded and I looked into a small room which had the prim neatness of Maud's uniform.

"Reena's is there," Anne made no move toward the other door.

I pounded on it.

"Who's there?" came a sullen croak.

"Miss Jansen, Reena. We need your help. The baby's missing. We—"

"Go away!" The croak swelled to a near shout. "Me—I'm not comin' outa here. Go 'way!"

And to all my attempts to enlist her aid she made no other answer. Defeated, we returned to the second floor. Then I urged Anne ahead of me down to the kitchen.

We were greeted by acrid smoke and the stench of burning. That minor crisis appeared to rouse Anne, who grabbed a pot holder and snatched a blackened pan with charred contents from the oven, conveying the mess to the sink. As far as I could judge, no one had been here since I left to take up Stuart's milk.

The back door was locked, the night chain in place. Beyond Reena's window, the snow was unbroken by any track.

Now Anne led, going back over my earlier route through the lower-floor rooms. It was not until we stood in the parlor, still holding its taint of fading flowers, that I spoke.

"What do you really know about Leslie Lowndes?"

Anne's head jerked as if the question had touched the spring of nightmare.

"She—she works at Gunniford's—she has something important to do in their import side. They moved that section out here to Ladensville two years ago. Hanno knows her. She had been overseas for Gunniford's and then promoted to this place. But she thought she might be sent to Europe, so she didn't want to rent an apartment until she was sure about that. She—she's friendly with Mr. Cantrell—"

"Worked overseas—" I repeated. Anne looked straight at me and I saw the icy fear awake in her eyes.

"Roderick!"

Her horror was so naked I hedged. "That is only a guess. We can't be sure."

Anne turned and ran from the room. I had to sprint to catch up with her as she reached for the phone with shaking hands.

"Police—" Her teeth were chattering so I could barely distinguish the words. "Must get the police."

"Listen." I caught her hands, held them in a way which I hope would be reassuring. "Colonel Rohmer is on his way here now. He should be arriving soon. Meanwhile I'm going to look out in the garden. We didn't hear any car leave—"

Anne seized upon that. "No—no car! Hurry—hurry!"

"You must wait for Colonel Rohmer," I told her. "Tell him what had happened and where I have gone."

"I will, oh, I will! But hurry—please hurry!"

I sped back to my room for coat and scarf, and then went down for my boots, making sure I had a flashlight in my pocket. Anne paced up and down the lower hall, her attention fixed on the front door. I thought I could safely leave her to follow orders.

A moment or two later I did find a trail. The side door had not been locked, and outside were rapidly filling smudges of footprints. I began to run. Then my feet slipped, spilling me forward so that the arm I flung out instinctively, to save myself from crashing on my face, gave me a numb wrist as I scrambled up again. I didn't want broken bones. I must be more careful, in spite of the tearing urgency building within me.

In a way I was responsible for this. If only I had not concealed the note from Irene. I had been warned by Mark to keep my eyes open, yet I had allowed this to happen! It was up to me to do all I could to find Stuart.

Leslie Lowndes, Leslie who had been abroad, who had admitted knowing Roderick, and so might have her own reason for wanting him dead. Leslie who had suggested the story of the two murderers. But what had led her to this last reckless action, drawing suspicion to herself, when, as far as I knew, she had been in the clear?

However, perhaps the police—Mark—had had suspicions not voiced to the rest of us. Leslie might have been pushed to the point where she believed only a desperate chance was left her. Was she planning to use Stuart as a bargaining point, a hostage? So much depended upon what kind of a person she really was.

I beamed my flashlight on the walk, following those evenly spaced prints which reminded me of my first visit to the Abbey. Had it been Leslie's trail then which had come out of the bushes? Leslie's wet boots I had found in the carriage house?

The walk reached that iron bench behind which I had taken cover. But this time the tracks did not head towards the yew-bordered burial plot, but the other way down which I had fled with Mark in pursuit—to the theater!

I took the precaution of snapping off my flashlight. I wanted no chance I might be seen from the building ahead. The street light, some distance away, awoke reflection to my right. As I had done before I used the wall of the building as a guide to the parking space. There was a car there—although the street gate was closed—a small sports car, its hood ridged with snow.

The theater building was dark, there was no sign of anyone about. I flashed my light at the license plate of the car. A New York one. I repeated the figures, trying to fix them in my memory. Whoever had brought it here must be inside—with Leslie.

Under my tentative push the main door swung open, and I crept into darkness. Though the area in which I now stood was dark, there was a dim glow at the far end. My eyes adjusting, I saw that this came from one end of a small stage. I must be in the auditorium of the long closed theater.

Hugging the right-hand wall, I made my way towards that light. Some trick of acoustics carried the murmur of voices and I hastened my crab's progress toward the stage. As a board creaked, I halted, my heart pounding. That sound had *not* come from beneath *my* feet.

The murmur continued. Pressed against the wall, I looked around, alert for that other lurker who might even now be converging on my own course.

Mark? Could it be Mark? But if he had gone to the house and listened to Anne he would not have had time enough—

I dared not believe in any ally here. Rather, I had to remain where I was and try to see that other. But what if I lingered too long and Leslie left—

My palms were wet, but my mouth felt dry, as I vacillated between going on and remaining where I was. A second creak out of the dark plucked at my nerves. Now I did see that other as a dark form arose above the level of the stage boards. It hunched there for a moment and then ran lightly, noiselessly, on. I caught a glimpse of what might be a masculine outline against that poor light before it vanished.

Able to breathe freely again, I resumed my journey towards the same goal, searching as best I could each pool of shadow for any other lurker. As I made the stage I could see large canvas flats leaning against the walls. Behind any one of those someone might lie in wait.

But I was more intent upon the voices, now clear, with not only the words but the tones of the speakers to be caught.

"—got to be here—" A man's hoarse whisper.

"You've had the better part of a week to find it!" My last doubt vanished. That was Leslie. Did she have Stuart with her?

"Are you even sure he hid it here?" Though Leslie spoke in a low voice, the other kept to that half-muffled whisper.

"Of course, he did. I told you how he stood right there and dared to tell me that the old lady knew everything. Because she had listened to him, she was willing to welcome him back into the family so he could now work her for all he wanted! I always said he could not be depended upon. If he saw it to his advantage he was willing to change sides."

"You've told me a good many things, my sweet, in

the years we have been associates. You're a very in-structive person."

I shivered, but not from the chill thrown out by these walls. Never, I thought, would I care to hear that whispering voice so addressing me.

"Oh, don't be stupid! This is serious. We're in luck tonight having the place free so we can give it a good going-over. It's here all right, Roderick boasted about that. He taunted me with it—"

"Just before you shot him? Your impatience on that occasion, my dear, still surprises me. Why shoot him before you had the manuscript in your pretty painted claws? Look at the amazing amount of trouble your impetuous action has caused. You have been too hasty by far—"

"As if I could have done anything else under the cir-cumstances! Even you would have admitted it, had you been here."

"But I wasn't here, was I, my dear? Because you were so very sure you could handle that obnoxious Roderick in your own practiced way. To that I agreed, though I had reservations even then. It was very short-sighted of me."

Again I shivered. The black threat in that whisper. Didn't Leslie hear it yet? The speaker was working towards some action more dangerous than mere words. And the voice—I could not place it—yet in a way it was vaguely familiar.

There followed a moment of silence before Leslie spoke.

"Just what are you hinting at?"

"That we both know you have a devious mind, my

sweet—have you not proved that many times in the past? Having watched with admiration your operations in our specialized field, I cannot help but wonder now if you have always been as frank with *me* as you professed to be. When one is adept in any particular action, it is so very easy to continue to use the same means to get any desired effect."

"That is not true!" Her denial was vehement and quick.

"I hope so, my dear, I very much hope so. Otherwise the consequences for us both might be distressing. Then you did not keep that rendezvous with Roderick to get the manuscript for yourself, but to—as one might say—toll him back to the path of duty?"

"Of course!"

"I wish I could believe you completely. I am desolated to discover it hard to summon up the necessary faith. Also—you have not yet made it plain to me why it is needful to withdraw from the field tonight—"

"You fool!" She had regained her poise. As if the other had, in his last speech, revealed some weakness she could turn to her own advantage. "They have a good suspect. But the case against her won't hold up too long under investigation. And Rohmer's snooping. When he learns a little more, how long do you suppose we will have?"

"Somebody will take care of Rohmer."

My heart pounded heavily at the cold and deadly promise of that.

Leslie laughed, an ugly sound. "So you have said before, so Paddy said, so Kauffman said. Do you want me to continue down the list of those brave souls who set out in the past to take care of Rohmer? He has a plant in the house already."

"Who?"

"That skinny old maid Jansen."

"But she only came Sunday—"

"Which means they tailed Roderick from New York and were ready with this plant if she were needed here. I know you are always inclined to underestimate the opposition lately, but that never pays."

"As you yourself have so aptly demonstrated in this case. Or are your superior gifts due to the fact you are one of the tougher sex? But now, may I call to your attention the fact that, short of taking up the flooring here—a task for which we have neither the tools nor the time—we have ripped this room apart, enough to prove that Roderick's cache does not exist. At least no longer exists. I would suggest that you put an end to this farce, which I no longer find amusing, and produce the envelope. I have no more time to waste."

"I don't know what you are talking about. And I promise you that they are not going to be too quick to close in on us." She laughed more softly. "I have taken precautions against that. I am sure they will be very much inclined to listen to any bargaining I suggest."

If Leslie had Stuart with her, he had made no sound. But those last remarks suggested that her present companion might not know she had taken the baby.

"The manuscript, my dear, where is it?" He did not seem interested in her hints. I heard feet move on an uncarpeted floor.

"I don't know what he did with it, and that is the truth."

"The which you would not probably tell if your life depended upon it. This time it does, sweet." The whisper he still held to made that threat sound even more drilling.

There was a moment of silence during which I shrank back against the wall. What about that other lurker who had come this way before me? Was he in hiding, listening too?

"Have you perhaps given it for safekeeping to the poodle dog—to little Gordon who runs to and fro for you, sits up and begs so prettily, and does just as you tell him? Does Cantrell have it now, holding it safe for his lily maid? So—" the whisper hissed, "you have again your little gun. How far-sighted of you, my dear. But I am not Roderick. I *know* all your games."

"Be very sure I'll use this if you come any closer!"

"How dramatic! Should I now cringe and slink away? But I am afraid I am going to fluff my cue. I came for the manuscript. It is the result of too much costly labor to allow you to keep it as a souvenir of a badly bungled job. Also, I am desolate, but it seems our partnership is now also dissolved, and I have a dislike for loose ends. Tell me, my dear, have you planned to set up business with Cantrell? Perhaps he is not as dull-witted as you hope. Sooner or later you would have been faced with another distressing scene—and then—exit poor poodle dog!"

"What I do in the future is my own affair."

"You are angry? Can it be that the poodle dog actually appeals to you, perhaps to the maternal instinct we are always told exists in every woman? But, my dear, then how your taste has declined. He is beneath your talents, far beneath them."

"You are being stupid now." Her voice rang with confidence. "If you think that Gordon Cantrell has any place in my future plans, that suggestion is—"

"Unworthy of me—or of you, my dear? So, and how did you plan to rid yourself of this clinging limpet?"

"When I leave here no one will ever find me—"

"So—" Again that warning hiss, with an inflection of triumph in it as if he had tricked her into an incriminating statement.

"Poor poodle dog. Then you did not after all entrust him with your secret."

"I tell you for the last time, I do not know where the manuscript is, if it is not here. This game is up anyway. It's time to cut our losses and get out. I promise you, I have insurance to get us a clear road."

" 'We'—'our'? The partnership is still in force, you believe? But that is impossible. I do not mind if you disappear from Cantrell's narrow little life. But I do object if you disappear from mine—until I have back what belongs to me. This has been a wearing conversation, and the hour is late. I have another appointment—"

I edged closer. It was suddenly very quiet.

Then—

"No!" Leslie's voice arose in a scream.

"But yes, my dear, yes!"

A thudding sound and then Leslie again, her voice now hysterical and broken—

"I shot you! I shot—"

Incredibly, the answer to that was a laugh, light and mocking. "But I do not fall nor bleed. I am not dead at all. Quite astonishing, is it not? Yet when you used that silenced gun on Roderick, he was safely out of your way at once. Now I put little trust in guns. People can wear—even in this day—armor, if they have suspicious minds. Cold steel is so much more sure—"

"Gordon!"

A dark shape arose to blot out the light in answer to that frantic call.

"So, my dear, you did not come alone to our meeting? Here is the poodle dog, waiting to provide the strong arms to dig my grave. Even as he helped you with Roderick. How provident of you!"

There came a second shot, but this one cracked like a thunderclap and before the echoes died away, the light laugh sounded.

"What a shock for you, Cantrell. Tonight it seems that I am the man who cannot be killed. But others can die—"

Leslie screamed, a high, tearing cry cut off in the middle—to be succeeded by a horrible bubbling choke. The light in the room snapped off. Then I heard the slam of a door. A moment later a motor was being gunned into life.

I stood where I was, too frightened at the moment to move. I could hear sounds from the other room and that bubbling continued. Then I forced myself to move on, snapped on my flashlight. The path of light from that swept ahead, over a floor heaped with clothing pulled from storage boxes. Then the beam fixed upon a scene I shall have to remember in nightmares for a long time to come.

Leslie lay in an angle between two of the boxes, her head and shoulders supported by them. From her throat poured a glistening flood of blood. Crouched on the floor by her, his eyes as wild as those of a hunted animal, was Gordon Cantrell.

As my light caught him, his lips drew back in a snarl and he hurled himself at me. At that moment I was frozen, unable to move.

My flashlight fell, to roll across the floor. Perhaps it was that which saved me from the full force of the attack he launched. An arm slammed along my thigh, hurling me back against the wall. One of his fists thudded into my ribs and I went down in a red haze of pain, only vaguely aware of what was about me.

Maybe I fainted, afterwards I was never sure. But when I pulled myself up, there was only one thought in my head—Stuart. Leslie must have brought him here. It was necessary to find him.

On my hands and knees I crawled across the floor to reclaim the flashlight which lay there—still lit. Then I got to my feet and flashed the beam about the walls to locate a light switch.

Shrinking, but knowing I must do it, I approached Leslie. The blood was not puddling on the floor, but the bubbling had stopped. Leslie's head had fallen forward so I could not see her face. Nor could I bring myself to touch her. I was sick, fighting to control a heaving stomach. So I made a wide circle around the body, searching as best I could. Nowhere was any sign of either Cantrell or Stuart.

I staggered back to the stage, using the flash recklessly now in long sweeps across the auditorium—light-
ing up all those empty seats.

Leslie must have brought him here. But where had
she left him? There was only one other place—the car
which had been parked outside. Leslie must have left
Stuart in that car!

14

I ran out of the theater into the thick swirl of a beginning blizzard. Wet snow clung to my eyelashes, plastered on my face and body. Even the beam of my flashlight was swallowed up by it.

Where the car had stood there was a bare spot now fast being covered with snow. While beyond the gate into the street was now open.

Stuart! The baby must have gone with the car. I had a last thin hope as I flashed the beam along the ground. But there was no tangle of blankets, no sign that the driver had jettisoned his passenger before he fled. Perhaps he did not even know of the child.

Police—only the police could deal with this!

There were lights on in the carriage house—closer now than the Abbey. Once more I began to run, slipping and sliding, fighting to keep on my feet. A car, only a dark blot in the fury of the storm, turned into the street as I stumbled up the Horvath drive.

Gordon—where had Gordon gone? I had forgotten him. Was he still back in the theater? I skidded to a halt—if he was—

I had shut out of my mind all but Stuart, in the way escaping the memory of Leslie as I had last seen her. It was the child who mattered. But if I went to the carriage house and Gordon was already there—what chance would he give me to call the police? Yet every minute I wasted—

The purr of a slowly moving car, the sound deadened by the snow, sounded close by. I glanced over my shoulder apprehensively. It had drawn even with the open gate to the theater, was stopping there. I lurched forward, a painful stitch in my side. Now the carriage house appeared to promise the most safety.

I slid across the pavement of the courtyard, saved myself from falling by clutching at a lamp post. A moment later, I raised a clatter with the knocker just as there came a shout from behind me.

"You there—stop!"

I clung to the knocker. There was no answer to my rapping in spite of the blaze of lights within. When I managed to face around I saw that my pursuer was a policeman.

"What's going on here? Why were you running?" he demanded.

"Baby—he's taken the baby! I want to call the police—"

"Well, I'm a policeman. Supposing you tell me all

about it. What's this about someone taking a baby, miss?"

I tried to build a coherent story in my mind. The important part was that there must be no loss of time. They had to find Stuart before the car would be beyond hope of pursuit.

I forced myself to speak slowly, and I hoped clearly. "A small sports car, the man driving it killed Leslie with—I think—a knife. He has the baby. And the license is a New York one." Out of my memory, I was actually able to pull the number digit by digit.

"All right, miss. I've got that. But you say someone is dead—killed—in there?" He pointed to the carriage house.

"No. Back in the old theater. But Stuart—it's most important to find him—now!"

"Sure." His hand closed gently about my elbow. He was guiding me back down the driveway. "I'm from a patrol car, miss. We can radio in about the baby. You come back and tell us all about it."

I looked to the house. Still no answer to my knocking. The car was parked just beyond the theater gate, and we headed towards it.

"You're just giving him more time to get away," I protested. "Please hurry to get the alarm out at once!"

"Sure, miss. Now if you just tell me exactly what has happened—"

"Leslie took Stuart out of his crib. I tracked her to the theater. She was quarreling with someone. They had been hunting something, and he accused her of taking it. She said—I think she was planning to use the baby as a hostage—there was a note—" I could not think straight. Because, even as I stared at the car white with snow, I saw now that red flood, heard that terrible bubbling again, and I began to shake.

"Who is the man, miss—you said 'he'?"

"I don't know, I never saw him—just heard them both. He—he was evil. Leslie didn't seem afraid of him—she should have been. Gordon was there, too, in hiding. The man—he drove off in the car with the New York license—" I repeated the number.

"Yes, miss. You told me that."

"And Stuart—I'm sure Leslie left the boy in the car. Because I couldn't find him inside when I looked."

Another policeman came down the theater drive and hurried to the car. I heard his voice inside, talking to the radio. Then he came over to us.

"Called it in, Del. This one's a dilly. Dame back there with her head half off—" Then he saw me and was abruptly silent.

"Send out an APB for a car with a New York license number—" My escort repeated it. "This lady says that the guy driving it did the knifing, and he has a kidnapped baby with him."

With a muffled exclamation the patrolman went back to the radio. Now the pressure on my elbow urged towards the theater. I was so tired. I wanted to just sit down somewhere and forget everything. But there was Stuart—and Mark. Where *was* Mark? At that moment I wanted him so much it was like a sharp pain in me.

Light streamed out through the open door. A moment later we stepped into the littered room. This must be a side door, the one through which the murderer had gone. One of the piles of plundered boxes hid Leslie's body. I was glad of that.

My companion walked cautiously forward. Under the light some of his high color faded. He stepped back hastily.

"Do we have to stay here?" I was sick, so very sick—

"What's beyond that?" He pointed to the other door.

"The stage and the auditorium. I wish you'd do something. He killed Leslie—what will he do to Stuart?"

"The car went out on the APB, miss. They'll be on the watch for it. And Homicide is on the way—"

"Mark!" I had not realized that I called his name aloud until I heard my own voice. If only Mark would come this whole crazy nightmare might end. He could find Stuart!

"Who, miss?"

"Mark, Colonel Rohmer. He was on his way here when all this happened. If you can just find him—please, find him!"

"Sure, miss." Again that soothing tone which I found increasingly irritating. But he made no move to leave. Where was Mark, or even Lieutenant Daniels?

I heard the howl of a siren.

"That'll be the sergeant now, miss."

"Leslie's dead. But Stuart is alive. That is the most important thing. That man who took him—he's the kind who would toss a baby right out of the car if he wanted to get rid of him. Why doesn't Mark come?"

There was a screech of brakes, and, as I looked out the door, I saw a number of men coming through the gate. There followed a hazy period of confusion, and then I found myself on one of the dusty theater seats facing Lieutenant Daniels, a Daniels with slit-narrow eyes and a set mouth.

"The baby—he took Stuart—" Surely Daniels who knew the Abbey and the inhabitants would understand the importance of what I was saying.

"You can't swear to that, Miss Jansen."

"Leslie brought him out of the house, he isn't here anywhere. So she must have left him in the car. And the man drove off in that car." I made my points with growing anger.

"Was Cantrell driving it?"

"No. Gordon was here after the man had left."

"Suppose you tell me the whole story again, Miss Jansen—from the beginning."

"I went down to the kitchen to get some warm milk for Stuart. I left his grandmother with him. Leslie was in the kitchen getting a meal. The front doorbell rang. We thought it was the nurse. Leslie went to let her in—she never came back." It was like trying to explain something to a child, I raged inwardly in exasperation—or to someone who did not understand plain English. I continued with my report of the discovery of the empty crib, the search of the house, my tracking the footprints to the theater, the quarrel I had overheard, all the rest.

"And you say that Cantrell left after this man you never saw?"

"He must have. I went to the carriage house because it was closer than the Abbey and I wanted to call the police. The lights were on but no one answered. Then the officer from the patrol car came."

"You did not recognize the voice of the man you didn't see?"

I felt as if I were one ache now, bruised by both weariness and worry. I could have screamed my answer at him. It took a lot of control to keep my voice normal.

"No, he just whispered—" There had been that odd sensation that there was something—but that was nothing concrete.

"Did Miss Lowndes call him by name?"

I forced myself to try to recall that conversation word by word. The menace conveyed in that whisper had the power to make me shiver even now.

"No."

"Too much to hope for—"

I looked around. Mark stood there at last. He was hatless, snow powdered in melting crystals on this thick cap of black hair.

"We can guess," he said to Daniels, "that it is tied up with the other matter. We'll have to play it my way."

"Mark!" I scrambled up, and my hands closed on his arm, which at that moment seemed the safest of anchors. "That man took Stuart. I'm positive!"

He nodded, which brought me a vast feeling of relief.

"There is an APB out on the car," Daniels said.

"He's on the run, and he has one bolt hole he doesn't know we've located. Get the state police and call Melborne, and tell him to bottle up the river."

"You're going down there?"

Once more Mark nodded. He had gently loosened my grip on his arm, but he still held my hand in his. It seemed to me that for the first time in hours I began to feel warm.

"We have this much in luck." He continued to Daniels. "I'm sure he doesn't know we've learned about the cottage. But his knowledge of the countryside is thorough. However, he may be warned off lesser-known roads because of the storm. We can get there, I think. How long ago did he leave?" Now he turned to me.

I could only shake my head. Time had not run in any pattern this night. It could have been thirty minutes, or an hour and thirty minutes. I did not know.

"The boys have been here about forty-five minutes," Daniels answered for me.

"Perhaps an hour then. And you've had no report on the car?"

"None so far."

"That means he headed straight for the river place. You send out the alarms. Meanwhile I'll get there as fast as I can."

He looked at me. "The lieutenant will see you back to—"

"No," I protested instantly. "You'll need me when you find Stuart. He's sick, remember?"

To my relief, he did not deny my help. When I slipped as we started toward the Abbey, he caught my arm and supported me until we reached the car parked under the Abbey portico. The windshield was plastered with wet snow, and he had to use the wiper before we dared start.

I hunched in the bucket seat. Visibility was very poor. This was a heavier storm than was usual—more like those my home state produced. If it kept on like this, traffic would be tied up.

The car skidded as we turned into the main thoroughfare. Mark grunted. Luckily traffic was light. Half a block away, a bus lumbered along at no more than a walking pace.

"Driving will be bad—" I hoped that that might hold up the man we pursued.

I wanted to ask where we were going, who Mark thought our quarry to be. Almost as if he read my mind he began to talk, with many pauses as he negotiated some turn or worked his way around stalled cars.

"We have to get into the river country. And the driving may be even worse there. But there is a speedboat at the cottage—"

"Please—who is he?"

To my surprise, Mark hesitated. "We have only a name so far—and we are sure that it is not the one he may be using now. He has played a very canny game for a good many years. We believe that he is the head of the ring—blackmail as well as the money-washing deal is all part of it. There are people 'above suspicion,' important enough to bring pressure to bear on authorities. This Newson has some of those in his pocket. He is a practiced manipulator. We cannot approach a lot of those we are suspicious of as his customers and accuse them of making deals—not without more proof than we have.

"He has been very clever indeed, dealing almost always through crooked channels which are set like the old espionage-cell patterns. That is—each man or woman he works through knows only one contact, and those near him may not know him at all except as a voice on the phone, or a note delivered by mail. Until tonight he has never taken one step out in the open. And why he did—it is hard to guess. Leslie Lowndes must have been a rare threat to him personally. He knows that his cover must be nearly perfect—perhaps he had to kill to protect that—"

"He accused her of holding out something," I said. "He thought she had double-crossed him."

"Still," Mark said slowly, "heretofore his cover has been more important to him than any loss. There must be some reason why—"

We were in the suburbs now, that part of town which was newly laid out to provide refuge from Washington for upper-income bureaucrats. Snow caked on the windshield in spite of the sweeps of the wipers. Twice Mark stopped to get out and push off the accumulation by hand. I looked at the clock on the dashboard—one! And the storm was not slacking. The headlights battled against the whirling snow curtain with little success. As we crawled on, I did not see how Mark could be sure of the division between road and sidewalks.

"Irene had nothing to do with it, had she? Why was Miss Elizabeth so certain that she did?"

"It turned out that she was only certain of the coat she saw—not the woman who wore it. I had a talk with her earlier tonight. She finally admitted that."

"That hideous plaid! Then perhaps Leslie—"

"Borrowed Irene's coat, yes. We don't know if she

did that intentionally for a disguise, or just because it happened to be near to hand. Irene had a habit of dropping her things around, according to Horvath."

Remembering the untidiness of her bedroom, I could agree.

"And Leslie could have poisoned the ginger, too, when it was left on the hall table. They all knew Emma's sensitivity to the delphinium seed."

"Maybe. But we still know very little about Leslie. And what would be her motive for that?"

"When she was quarreling, she and that man, she said something about Roderick having told Mrs. Horvath everything in exchange for a deal for himself."

"That fits—partly. Whew!" His exclamation was for the fury of the wind-driven snow building a white wall about the car. It was very difficult now to see. Our speed was a crawl as Mark centered all his attention on the driving. He made a slow turn to the left under a traffic light so plastered with snow that only a faint glimmer of red and green showed. Moving traffic had vanished—though cars had pulled to the curbs, some abandoned far enough out to near block our passage.

I tried to see through the side window. The car lurched and slid while Mark fought the skid. We ended with a jar against a buried curb. For a moment I thought we were finished, but Mark maneuvered us on with a skill which earned my fullest admiration. Outwardly he showed no trace of agitation though I could guess what a strain this progress was.

"Is it much farther?"

"I could answer that better," came his clipped reply, "if I knew just where we were now."

Ahead was another glint of light—red—and it was down low, in the center of the road. Mark pounded on the windshield with his fist, dislodging a heavy clot of snow. Now we could see it was a warning lantern.

"Must be a smash-up." Mark slowed to a complete stop and opened his door. I wondered if the man we followed had come to such an end.

Mark disappeared into the whirl of snow. Flakes, shifting in through the half-opened door, blew inside my coat collar. With an effort I could just barely see figures moving ahead. I got out—unable to just sit still and wait.

Snow worked in over the tops of my boots, melting against my shivering legs. I trudged on to where headlights of cars fought the storm and there was a cluster of men.

"You can't make it without chains, not down the river road—" A masculine voice arose above the hiss of the falling snow. "We're turning everyone back."

Even at this distance I was able to identify the sound of Mark's voice, though I could not make out the words.

"Yes, sir, we got that APB. But the road—"

Again a murmur from Mark as I moved into the lantern light.

"Who's that? Lord, it's a woman!"

I disregarded the implied disapproval in that. "Mark, can't we go on? Has there been any news about the car?"

He came closer. "As far as they know he got through before the road started to drift and they set up this block. They're going to try to send a patrol car through, one with snow tires—"

"Can we go with them?"

He hesitated. "I'm going. But—"

"Mark, what about Stuart? Can any of you manage a sick baby?"

I was sure that the man who had dealt with Leslie was not going to surrender tamely. The police might forget Stuart—or not be able to get to him in time.

"They are not even sure they can make it."

However, when we walked around the barrier I was one of the party who crowded into the patrol car. I pushed as far as I could into one corner of the rear seat, trying not to look at the ugly weapon the trooper beside me balanced across his knees. Mark was in front to direct our course.

Did I doze? I cannot remember the rest of our journey clearly. I roused only when we came to a stop.

"There's no getting down the lane."

"No, but your car can block if he decided to run."

Mark was interrupted by a squawking, which jerked me fully alert. Through the screech of static a disembodied voice repeated a weird jumble of words. Mark gave an exclamation of satisfaction.

"He didn't try for the boat anyway. Now this is the only way out for him."

"Can't be too sure," the driver objected. "Sure, they may have the river blocked off. But he can try cross-country—the Lammer Road cuts through not too far north."

"The weather's against that. And he doesn't know we are on to this hideout—or at least he didn't at the last report. Erica." He turned to me. "That house is a quarter of a mile in. You stay here. When we find the child, we'll send him out to you at once. In the meantime—stay here!"

They strode away into the storm giving me no time to protest. The wind had fallen and the snow began to lessen. Now a moon crept warily out to send a white glitter across the drifts. Those lay in waves with fence posts rearing out of them to mark the edge of a field. As I watched, I saw that the men did not keep to the lane. Instead, they followed devious paths, working from one clump of half-buried brush to the next. There were no lights ahead, no indication that the house Mark mentioned even existed.

I waited until they were well gone and then got out of the car. It was impossible for me to sit still. My nerves urged me into action.

The snow lay deep, above the tops of my boots, caking on the skirts of my coat and on the pants under it. About me, the few flakes still falling glittered. All at once, in spite of weariness, of the sickening fear and tension of the past few hours, I felt invincible.

It was as if I knew that, like a story with melodramatic opening chapters, there would be a happy, or at least a peaceful, ending. I paused, panting with the effort the fighting of drifts cost me. Clouds were again drifting across the moon. Once more flakes of snow fluttered more thickly through the air.

15

I suddenly realized that I must be very noticeable here in the open. So I plowed from what must be the center of the snow-concealed lane toward a windbreak of trees. There were no lights or sounds. We might be in the deserted country. Those before me had disappeared. I pushed doggedly on. To stay behind bred fear. The line of firs I followed changed their course to become the edge of a clearing.

There stood a one-story ranch house, the snow before it unbroken, as far as I could see, by any tracks. Might Mark have been wrong? The appearance suggested that the place was unoccupied. I kept within the screen of trees and angled around toward the side and back of the house. It was when I had approached that portion of the building that I saw the car standing in the open. All my doubts vanished. Even in this limited light, I was sure I saw the same one which had been parked by the theater.

Stuart? Could he still be in there—perhaps undiscovered? Shifting my weight from one cold-numbed foot to the other I surveyed what lay ahead, trying to make sure I could reach the car unseen. To the right stood a clump of snow-laden bushes, beyond those the wall of what must be a carport. But the car itself was in the open.

A figure moving along the side of the house. One of the troopers—Mark? No, dead-white clothing made the newcomer near invisible, even his head was so covered. He could only be clearly seen when he moved before the car or the bulk of the house.

Then the shadow-man went on into the carport and came out, a large can in one hand. Setting that down, he pulled a blanketed bundle out of the car.

"Stuart!"

I hoped that bitten-off cry had not betrayed me. But he did not turn to look in my direction. The ski mask gave him a sinister appearance, as he carried the bundle a few feet away from the car and laid it down in the snow. He might have been getting rid of some unwanted trash. Returning, he picked up the can and began to dribble the contents across the car, and then in a trail back towards the carport and the house.

The smell of gasoline was suddenly strong. I readied myself for a dash. When the masked arsonist disappeared in the carport, I could wait no longer. Floundering through the snow, I reached that bundle. The baby made no sound as I gathered him up awkwardly. I worked a glove off one hand by using my teeth, and I touched the soft flesh of a small cheek. Warm—too warm!

I fled back into the shadow of the bushes, reaching my flimsy cover not a moment too soon. There was a stir in the carport. Stuart held against me tightly. I pushed back as far as I could among the bushes. That other came up to the car. There was a spurt of flame as small as might be made by a lighter.

"Hold it!"

Stuart whimpered. I must have tightened my grip still more in reaction to that sharp order.

With the speed of a hunting cat, the man hurled from him that spark of light he was holding. A brilliant flash followed and flames roared up, creating in an instant a wall of fire with the car at its core.

I screamed and struggled to retreat as the tongues of flame billowed out. More fire was engulfing the house.

There followed the crack of a shot. I stumbled and went down on my knees in the snow. Stuart cried and squirmed, but I pulled around until I could see the scene, now well lighted by the fire.

Mark, two of the troopers, were charging towards the fire itself. There were shouts, more shots. Rigid with such terror as I had never known, I saw the men driven back by the heat of that fire.

I could not get to my feet. I was too weak with fear. One of the troopers jerked, then staggered forward into the very edge of the fire. Mark darted in as the flames sent out a lashing red tongue. He grabbed at the wavering man, dragged him back. Not a moment too soon.

For there was an explosion from the interior of the house, blinding me, deafening me, too, with its roar.

Debris spun through the air. I choked in the wave of fumes carried outward from that source.

I blinked. Stuart was wailing now, but I could hear his cries only as if they came from a long distance away. Dimly I saw Mark being helped to his feet, other men bending over the fallen trooper.

Shots again—very faint, though. Was my hearing so impaired that it reduced them so? Mark shook off the hands of those who had aided him up. Now he made straight for the bushes where I sheltered.

"Come on—" The harshness of his voice had no power to hurt me. As long as he was standing there, apparently unhurt—not dead, not injured—nothing else mattered.

"I can't." I had to admit the humilating truth. "I don't think my legs will hold me."

He stopped and took the struggling baby out of my arms, passing the child to one of the troopers who had followed him. Then he pulled me up in turn.

"There goes the house!" the trooper cried.

I discovered I could move, even if I tottered, for Mark jerked me back, pulling me along at an unsteady run. There followed a second explosion.

"Lord, he must have tapped an oil well for a blaze like that!" The trooper panted. "Or else he had explosives planted. By way—"

"Of a cover," Mark finished.

I looked back over my shoulder. The house was a mass of seething flame, which the wind, once more driving snow before it, sent out in ragged banners behind us. There was a snapping crackle. One of the firs had caught.

"Keep going!" the trooper urged. Over his shoulder, eyes wide in his pinched face, Stuart was staring at the fire. He had stopped crying; perhaps he was shocked beyond it now.

"Nothing more we can do here." One of the other officers joined us. "As far as we can tell, nothing—or no one—got out of that!"

"Don't be too sure," Mark snapped. "That fire was meant to be a cover—perhaps for escape. The man we're after is not the kind to see going out in a funeral pyre would advance his plans any."

"Don't worry, we have patrols out. And I'll call in for more help on the car radio."

I stumbled continually, but Mark was always there. There was a third and final explosion, sending me closer to my companion in flight.

"You—you aren't hurt—getting that trooper out?" I found breath enough to ask at last.

"Just singed a little. But what were you doing there? I told you to stay in the car."

Something in his voice raised a shadow of my old antagonism—which I had so long cultivated for a shield.

"He—he just laid Stuart in the snow. If I hadn't gotten him away when I did, the fire would have reached him."

For perhaps the length of three strides Mark had no answer. When he did I was not alert enough to analyze the alteration in his tone.

"Cold-blooded. Yes, that would be part of it. It won't be long now—there's the car."

I felt like a sleepwalker, in one of those agonizing

dreams where one has to run before menaces while also entrapped in some substance like thick syrup. Once at the car I pulled myself into the corner of the back seat and held out my arms for Stuart. With a sniffling cry he clung to me, and I pulled the blankets as tightly as I could about him, hoping he might go off to sleep. Mark settled beside me and I was grateful for his company. They had trouble turning the patrol car—but they finally managed to fight a path through the drifts. Only the driver was with us—the others lingered on guard. I found my head was resting on Mark's shoulder and I only raised it when we came once more to the signal lantern at the barricade.

"Mark—did he—did he—" I ventured.

"I don't know." He answered my unfinished question. "There's always a chance. That's why I've got to make sure—" His voice trailed off as he drew away from me to get out. My arms felt numb under Stuart's weight, and my protest against Mark's going came seconds too late. I heard only a few words from outside.

"—yes, sir. We'll drive her straight there. You needn't worry."

"Mark!" But he was gone. My head flopped back and the red lantern light blurred. I was left in a cold loneliness which made me want to cry, save that I was too tired to raise a single tear.

Stuart began to fuss. I roused enough to pat him in what was, I hoped, a comforting fashion. We must be nearing town. I could see houses in the dim light of early morning. And I summoned voice enough to ask:

"Where are we going?"

"Feeling better, miss? The colonel said to take you straight home."

Home? To New Hampshire? For a crazy moment or two I thought longingly of that safe, warm, tidy place which had been my stronghold after I had sold Aunt Otilda's old house. Then I remembered—"home" now meant the Abbey. And that was no home for me.

"And Colonel Rohmer?"

"He stayed to see to things, miss. He'll have to have a doc look at his face, too—"

"His face!" I jerked upright, fully awake. "What's wrong with his face?"

"He got scorched when he dragged Hodgens out. Not too bad, miss. Don't you worry about it. There's an ambulance going out. They were sure lucky. Got away before the big explosion hit. A couple of minutes more and they both might have bought it, but good. Hey, they got a road crew out—that's going to help things a lot."

The trooper stopped the car. Now he leaned forward to exchange greetings through a hastily lowered window with another policeman. There was a snowplow nearby.

It was fully day by the time we reached the Austin house. Our car pulled to a stop under the portico and the trooper got out to ring the bell before he came to open the car door for me.

"Want me to take the baby, miss?"

I laughed shakily. "You'd better. I'm not sure I can even manage for myself."

Someone brushed past the trooper. Irene Frimsbee,

her face white and haunted, her hair in crazy witchlocks about her face, seized the baby.

"Stuart!" Her voice was hoarse, as if she had used it too much for a long time. "Stuart!" With him in her arms, she turned and ran back inside.

"That the kid's mother?"

"Yes. She must have been nearly crazy. Thank you for the ride back." It sounded as if I were thanking a stranger for a lift. But it was hard to think straight. All I wanted was to reach my own room.

"No trouble, miss." He sketched a salute.

I made it to the door. There I saw Lieutenant Daniels—or did I only imagine that? But I kept putting one foot before another until I reached the stairs.

"Can I help you?" I did not turn my head to see who had asked that. Any unnecessary movement, I felt, might upset my balance and I would collapse altogether.

"I am going to bed," I said distinctly, "and perhaps I shall stay there forever."

My hand on the banister helped to pull me up. I locked the door of my room behind me, and for the first time in my disciplined life I shed my clothing, to leave it in a wet tangle on the floor. Too tired to pull on a nightgown, I dragged my robe about me and burrowed into the bed, to fall into exhausted slumber.

I sat up groggily in a gray, shadowed room and gave a cry as the walls appeared to ripple and the bed sway under me. While holding tight to fistfuls of covers in a fight against the vertigo, I heard a pounding on my door, the sound which must have roused me.

A muffled voice called, and the rapping increased in tempo. Cautiously I slid to the edge of the bed, working my way along until I could hold the foot. With that support I got to my feet, wavered on to catch at a chair back, and finally reached the door. It was largely hunger, I decided—I was simply weak from hunger.

"Oh, shut up!" I snapped at the unseen making that racket. "I'm coming as fast as I can!"

I unlocked the door but opened it only a crack. Anne Frimsbee stood there. She once more looked arrogant and assured.

"Miss Jansen, Lieutenant Daniels—we are all waiting."

"For what?" I found it necessary to cling to the edge of the door. The floor had an annoying tendency to rise and fall, as if I were on board ship.

"For you."

"I don't know what you mean, and I am not at all well. What time is it anyway?"

She glanced at her watch. "Five-thirty."

"And what day?"

She gasped. "Why—Sunday, of course."

"I haven't had anything to eat since our tea yesterday, Mrs. Frimsbee. First things first. Now I don't think I have the strength to crawl down stairs."

"Oh." Apparently I had made some impression on her. As one who must be always fighting a grim battle between an interest in food and her figure, she could understand a plea of starvation. "I'll just slip down and get you something. A sandwich—"

Was it the subject of food which had induced this softening of her attitude? I did not care. As I turned away, the sight of those garments on the floor shocked me into greater effort. The events of early morning now seemed unreal. Had it all been a nightmare? But the acrid scent of smoke clung to my coat, and melted snow weighted the pants.

I was pulling on stockings, when a second tap at the door announced the arrival of Anne with a tray. "Ham." She indicated a rather ragged-looking sandwich. "That other one is honey butter, Stuart's favorite."

"How is Stuart?"

"Dr. Bains says he will be all right. But Irene finally agreed that they could take him to the hospital." She did not mention my efforts in his behalf, and I saw no reason to remind her.

I wolfed the sandwich, drank the lukewarm tea in the cup, before I asked:

"Why does Lieutenant Daniels want to see me?"

As if my words had summoned the law, a rap at the unlatched door sent it open and I saw the sergeant's somewhat embarrassed face.

"We're—"

"Waiting. Yes, I know, Sergeant. But if you want me you'll have to continue to wait for a few minutes. I'm now eating last night's dinner, and today's meals all in one."

Perversely I refused to be hurried. Where once I had had an uneasy reaction to the law, a searching of conscience, now I discovered a detachment which armored me so I might finish every crumb before I joined the gathering in the parlor.

There were important gaps in that fidgeting assembly. No Miss Austin dominated the company, Leslie's sleek elegance was missing. I flinched from remembering Leslie as I had seen her last.

Preston Donner sat alone on a stiff settee, his customary gray suit in contrast to the wine velvet of its upholstery. His face was drawn and had a tinge of the same grayness as his clothing. He looked up at my coming, and produced a twitch of the lips which he might intend as a polite smile. But there was an effort even in so small this acknowledgment of my presence, as if some great weariness sapped his strength.

I was tempted to take a seat beside him, aware as ever of that courtesy, which always awoke in me a feeling of security, born as it was from the familiar manners of Aunt Otilda's world. Still there was something about him now, as if he had made an effort to disengage himself from the others, which warned me off. His eyes had not met mine for long. Rather, they had slid past me quickly, and there had been no welcome in those.

Hanno Horvath, a black band decorously stitched about the sleeve of his brown tweed jacket, arose from a chair too small for his leonine bulk and nodded his head in my direction. His countenance was as stubbornly somber as ever.

A little beyond him, Irene perched on a straight backed seat as if arrested in mid-flight. Her unwillingness to be there was plain. Only Anne Frimsbee had any semblance of ease, her plump feet planted on a footstool, her hands loosely folded, as if she were a spectator at a play she had been assured would be fascinating.

I was not, after all, last to arrive. For I had no more than sat down when the Sergeant ushered in two others. Theodosia halted just within the doorway. Under her makeup she looked not only sick but aged, her lower lip caught between her teeth as if to stifle a protest pride would not permit her to utter. Though Blake and Gordon flanked her, she had a strange air of being alone.

Sensing her isolation, I could not stand it. I went to her and drew her with me to another settee, facing Donner's. She came docilely enough, never glancing at the two who had entered with her.

Gordon Cantrell looked as frozen as his wife. That youthful air which had supplied much of his charm had vanished. The face now so exposed was weak and the eyes glassy. He stood where he was until Blake near pushed him into a chair. Then the sergeant handed the lieutenant, who stood on the edge of the hearth, a large manuscript envelope.

"It was there right enough, sir. Under the driver's seat in the car."

"How careless." Daniel's voice held a jaunty ring, in bitter contrast to the uneasy atmosphere of the room.

Theodosia's hand fell on the cushion between us, and I covered it with my own, in a gesture I hoped would be reassuring. But the lieutenant, to my surprise, did not continue. It was Hanno Horvath who asked:

"Is that what you have been hunting, then?"

"Yes."

"And it is a forgery? Made to deceive my aunt?"

"We shall have to let the experts decide that. However, judging by the past deals this group has pulled, it will probably be bogus. What about it, Mr. Donner?" Daniels opened the envelope, took out some sheets of plastic, each of which enclosed a page of paper, yellow, worn at the edges, apparently old. He handed one to the expert in old books. "What's the chance of this being the real thing?"

Preston Donner left the sheet lying on his knees as he brought out reading glasses and put them on. Something, his inner warmth, which had drawn me to him at our first meeting, had been snuffed out. He was tired, and looked old now, wearing his years heavily. When he held the sheet closer to the lamp, his hand shook a little. His precise voice was low-pitched—it sounded different—

"Without further tests I cannot give any opinion, Lieutenant. If this should prove authentic it would be close to priceless for the right collector. The first draft of *Pride and Prejudice* as was written under the title of *First Impressions*. I think a great deal could be asked for it. However, I would require some very rigid tests." He passed back the sheet, almost as if he wanted it out of his hands.

"How much *did* you expect to get?" Daniels asked Gordon Cantrell in a whip-crack voice.

Gordon's expression—or rather lack of one—did not change. "I didn't hide it, if that's what you mean. I knew nothing about it."

"Did you ever consider, Lieutenant—" Theodosia's

hand in mine twitched as she spoke, but her voice was perfectly even—"that he may be telling the truth? We never kept the garage locked."

"So that anyone might have used your car for a hiding place without your knowledge? That is naturally the explanation Mr. Cantrell is going to use. But we have ways of checking. Now." This time he swung upon Hanno Horvath. "You are the one who introduced the Lowndes woman into the house. Were you aware of her background—that she had a legitimate claim on the Austins?"

"What!" Anne Frimsbee lost her pose of spectator. She stiffened, her small eyes open to their widest extent. "What claim could she possibly have on us?"

Daniels paid her no attention. He was still eyeing Hanno, as if to force the answer he wanted out of the big young man. "Did you know that she was not Miss Lowndes at all?"

"I knew she was married—and divorced, if that's what you mean." Hanno's calm remained unruffled. "She was a valued assistant in the company—I had known her overseas. There was no reason for me to question what she told me concerning her past. But—" He suddenly shot an openly malicious glance at Gordon Cantrell. "I was by no means her only dupe—nor her latest. She used me to introduce her around here. But I was only one of her men. And of me she wanted comparatively little. You can check that, too—you probably have—and you know what I say is true."

"Lieutenant!" Anne Frimsbee interrupted for the second time. "I want you to explain just what you mean by saying that Leslie Lowndes had some sort of a claim on my family!"

"Not Leslie Lowndes," he corrected, "Leslie—Blackmur."

16

The only definite reaction I could see came from Anne. Her mouth dropped a little open—she might be gasping at some effrontery.

"Elinor Austin," Daniels continued, "married Blackmur, your father's secretary. He was killed in a car accident three years later. Leslie was the only child of that marriage."

Anne bristled. "We know nothing about that," she declared shrilly. "My father was very angry with Elinor. She deceived him shamefully. We never heard from her after she eloped with Harlon Blackmur. Father made us all promise never to have any contact with her." She paused—then she asked: "Is Elinor still living?"

Daniels shook his head. "Your sister died, Mrs. Frimsbee. She was near destitute. She had been unable to work for some time prior to her death." He glanced around the room as if he were assessing it and the scale of life it represented.

Its furnishings were, of course, well out of date. The one-time opulance was gone, well dulled by time. But it still had the atmosphere of security and solid comfort which had impressed me. This whole house was a symbol of one-time wealth, and not all of that glamour had been dissipated.

"The circumstances under which Mrs. Blackmur died appear to have embittered her daughter. I think she instigated this particular deal in a desire to bleed from the Austins some of the money which she thought should have been used for her mother, knowing also if she were discovered it would make a scandal for the family."

"This was all *her* plan then?" demanded Anne, who appeared to consider herself spokesperson for the company.

"We cannot be sure—there are loose ends. But as far as we can discover she met Roderick in Europe and pumped him about the family. Perhaps she had nothing definite in mind then. She may have just been looking for something to use to her advantage. She had apparently worked with Newson from time to time. He was always on the lookout for just such a situation as Dr. Edwards' will and the trust fund.

"Provided with what Roderick could tell her, she saw not only a chance to score off the family she hated, but to give Newson an opening over here—"

"Who is Newson?" Hanno Horvath asked.

"That is a good question," Daniels nodded. "He is

behind this present trouble, but it is certainly not his first deal by any means. For some years he has run rackets dealing with faked antiques. Anyway, Leslie settled in here. Then she had to deal with Mrs. Horvath, who had been made the trustee."

"Not so easy, that," Hanno commented. "Miss Emma was not the type to be influenced by a woman, especially one of Leslie's sort. They were really too much alike, ready to ride over those who tried to oppose them. Was that why Roderick was brought in—to play the penitent and snare Miss Emma's interest? This Newson—I suppose he could not play the charmer's role?"

"Newson made a point ordinarily of keeping away from any action in progress."

"Always Newson—" Hanno glanced around at our company. "Now I wonder—" He hesitated and then was silent for a moment before he changed the subject.

"Was Roderick penitent? Did he come to charm Aunt Emma, then?" Hanno did not look at Gordon Cantrell, but there was something spiteful in his tone.

"We can't tell about that now. It may be that Leslie made some slip, and Roderick arrived purely on his own to do some fishing in troubled waters. It was apparently the sort of thing which would draw him."

"May we guess that once here Roderick chose to play his own hand?" Hanno asked. "Then Leslie disposed of him? She was never one, I think, to tolerate a double-cross. But why the trick with the coffin?"

Daniels now turned directly to Gordon. "Suppose you explain. You had a part in that, didn't you?"

"Leave me alone!"

Theodosia's hand turned in mine and gripped so tightly I almost cried out. She was rigid, watching Daniels as one might watch a growing menace.

"You're lucky," Daniels said, "that there is a witness to get you off the hook for Leslie's murder. Or you might have had to answer some questions about that also—"

"Shut up!" Gordon was on his feet, his face an ugly mask of hate and weak anger. "Shut up! I'm not going to listen to this—" He turned on his heel and left the room.

The lieutenant made a signal, and Blake was quick to follow Cantrell. Theodosia loosed her grip on me and arose.

"Is he under arrest?" she asked in a voice so remote that she might have been inquiring about the weather.

"He may be—"

"I believe I have the right to call a lawyer for him."

"True, Mrs. Cantrell."

It seemed to me that she winced when he called her by that name. But she held her head high, and no shadow of any emotion was visible on her face.

"May I do so now?" She had already half-turned to the door. Someone stood there—my hand clenched on the arm of the settee.

It was Mark, his dark face as impassive as ever. But there was a strip of gauze taped over one cheek.

Beyond me someone moved, a swift movement, quickly checked. Theodosia stepped aside and he came in to stand beside Daniels. From his pocket, he brought out what looked like an oversized wallet.

"Newson is a careful man," he announced, "but he

has not been involved in any direct action for some time. He had, he thought, graduated to the place where he would be always the planner, not the doer. But he did keep a personal file." Mark touched the wallet he had laid beside the sheets of disputed manuscript. "He could believe he had escaped us—that dodge of wearing a white ski suit and mask, of lying out in the snow until the hunt had spread beyond him and then using *our* tracks to get out—clever. It did win him time which was what he wanted. Unfortunately—fire sometimes plays freaky tricks. This was not destroyed."

The last sentence was directed to only one of us. My gasp of sudden understanding was covered by that other's voice, colorless, different in tone.

Just as Preston Donner had also vanished before our eyes, the man in gray had dropped that personality like a worn coat. He who sat across from me was a stranger I would have sworn I did not know—nor had I. It was not that he had been disguised, in the general sense. It was rather as if by some inner change of will he could emerge another person in an instant.

"A pity." His voice was different and I again gasped—how could he have so learned to alter that? This was the speaker I had heard with Leslie—even though he did not whisper now. "You are right."

He and Mark might have been alone in the room.

"I made the error of taking a hand in the action myself. The sign of senility, I suppose—"

Anne Frimsbee started out of her chair.

"Preston!" Her voice was pure protest. "Why—"

He shrugged and smiled. No more Donner. The protective coloring of the rather fussy gentleman, perhaps in his sixties, had entirely sloughed away. Ruthlessness and sharpness broke through outward mask of gentility.

"Money, my dear Anne. Money—and of course a certain interest, a gambler's interest, if you will. I am afraid I betrayed my cloven hoof, which is also my downfall, in my desire to show that I could still pull off a trick such as this. With me it is not altogether the money—it is also the game, and of course the things money can buy. Certain comforts, little luxuries, grow more important as one ages. Then also—one begins to wonder if one is slipping—if one *can* still match one's subordinates. Pride goes before a fall—I am afraid I allowed pride to rule my judgment.

"Donner has been a useful role over a good many years, one of my better other selves. I have been proud of Donner in the past. And this seemed just the exploit for him. Emma would have accepted my verdict on any manuscript. It was as if I were taking a sabbatical here—able to devote my time meanwhile to another idea—" He laughed. "But it is not necessary to go into all that. That piece of planning, alas, now may never come to fruition. But my cover was very good—ah, pride speaking again!" He shook his head. "I must learn to note my weaknesses. Anyway, Emma came to me at once when Roderick first approached her.

"Up to that time I was not aware of all the ramifications of Leslie's little deal." Now his face took on grim tightness. "I knew of the trust, of course, and I had considered to myself about dipping into it. But my final decision had been made that the return might be too small to bother with. Leslie came to me here. She had earlier suborned one of my technical assistants—an artist, a vertible artist in forgery. She told me her little tale.

"Leslie wanted my help. I was at loose ends for a space before my own plan would develop. I agreed. She knew my word meant a quick sale. With Miss Emma growing older, there was a chance she might die and the trust be put under more discerning control. I had kept Donner as an alternate personality for a good many years—Edward Austin was not the only client who trusted him implicitly. I had made my position above suspicion. So I agreed in a moment of weakness—"

"You did not bargain on murder," Mark commented. "Then you were involved—"

"True. I have ever eschewed any close touch with violence."

"But this time—"

Donner or Newson nodded. "I have taken care of my people. They know I abhor both violence and any double-cross. Leslie plunged me into murder, then dared to refuse me the evidence which I must destroy to cover us." He nodded to the manuscript pages. "With those out of the way—" He shrugged. "Then—there was other evidence—which I was able to handle better. But she had visions of blackmail." His smile now was only a baring of teeth. "You may have that." He gestured to the wallet. "But I assure you that is nothing beside what I took care to see go up in flames last night!"

"Shall we go?" Daniels moved towards Donner. The

man, with a second shrug, arose and started to the door.

Mark made no move to follow. I wanted to go to him, assure myself that he had taken no worse hurt than the one he showed. Theodosia now left—and I, suddenly unsure as to why, followed her.

"Where's the phone?" she asked.

I took her down the hall.

"Do you know who to call?"

"John Billings, I suppose. He doesn't take—criminal cases. But he ought to be able to advise me." She went to dial. As I started away, she called over her shoulder:

"Please wait—"

"Mr. Billings? Not there? Have him call—" She gave the number of the carriage-house phone. "It is urgent."

Then she asked me a question I was not prepared to answer.

"What is there between you and Colonel Rohmer, Erica?"

"Nothing." I made my answer as firm as I could. "We knew each other some years ago. But I have not seen him until now—"

"He has influence, I would judge. Oh, I know Gordon is worthless. I've known for years that he played around." She had shaded her eyes with her hand, but there was no betraying note in her voice. "It's because he's weak that I can't just walk out on him now. If I did that I'd put myself on his level."

"But—"

"But I can't go on with him? Is that what you are

too polite to ask, Erica? Well, maybe that's true. I'll have to make sure. Only what I do now and what I shall decide to do later, those are two different things. Gordon is innocent of murder. Daniels will probably arrest him—but there's other ties in this. Donner—Newson—he seems to be more important. Maybe Mark Rohmer can do something, if Gordon turns state's evidence. Will you speak to him and find out, Erica?"

I did not want to. But I did not know myself very well anymore. Last night I seemed to have passed some barrier and come out into a new existence. I was frightened—more than a little. This was too intense—this feeling inside me now.

"Theodosia." I selected my words with care, to make what I was saying convincing not only to her but to myself: "To tell you the truth, we are not on friendly terms. I had ample proof years ago that I meant nothing to him. And maybe if I tried to speak for Gordon, the very fact that *I* was the one to do it might prejudice him."

Theodosia was staring at me.

"You are either a stupid liar or a blind fool!" Her voice was hot with anger, and she pushed past me as if I had ceased to exist.

Her response shook me. I wanted now to assure her that I would do what I could for Gordon—not that it would help. But she was already gone—out the back way towards the door which gave on the garden walk.

I heard steps behind me. Mark, and over his arm a coat. Not mine, but he held it for me to slip on. I gathered up a scarf trailing over the table where the tin of ginger had once stood. The experiences of the past twenty-four hours had done nothing to enhance my claim to any looks. But I knew that I must go with Mark and face squarely what lay between us, since he had chosen this way.

As he climbed in the waiting car, I caught a glimpse of Anne Frimsbee at the door. Then we were on our way, and I could not suppress a sigh of relief.

"What were you doing on Saturday, the twenty-fourth of August—need I say the year?"

I had expected anything but such a forthright and instant attack. But I had an answer which arose as if I had framed it ahead to be used on just this occasion:

"I might ask you the same thing!"

Emboldened at my ability to meet his first sortie, I turned my head a little to catch a glimpse of his dark face. But I only saw the bandage.

"Mark—that burn—how bad is it?"

"Nothing to shed tears over."

As if I were, I had, I told myself furiously. No, I would not give him advantage by again showing any concern. We drove in silence along the snowy street. Then I guessed Mark's chosen destination and I was bitterly angry.

He pulled in at the inn. I hoped it would be closed because of the weather. But his perverse luck held and we were ushered into the dining room where we were, at this hour, the only guests. It was just the same. Only then it had been summer—now it was winter.

"You have no right to do this!" I was goaded into speech as the waiter left us.

"Perhaps not." His ready agreement, when I expected the opposite, was disconcerting. "There is never any harm in trying, though. What did happen on that Saturday, Erica?"

I forced myself to meet his eyes as stonily as I could.

"You already know."

"I thought I might have—your dear Aunt Otilda's influence, I suppose. Did she succeed in making you believe that you shouldn't marry out of your own race—that to take up with me was a shame and disgrace?"

"Mark!" I was shocked out of my defense. If he believed *that*—which had never occurred to me! But no, that must have been *his* form of defense—if he needed any. We both knew the real truth.

"I know," he continued dispassionately, "that your aunt made you afraid of every honest emotion a woman might experience, but I didn't think she could keep you prisoner in her web forever, not if you were the person you could be. *Was* it that I am an Indian, Erica? Or just that I am a man, and so the enemy as far as the Aunt Otildas of the world are concerned."

"It was your wife. You can't deny I saw you both together—you looked straight at me—" I was lost to all pride at last.

His eagle face did not change. Instead he said very softly:

"So that was it. Without allowing me a chance at any explanation, you jumped to the worst conclusion. I think you wanted it that way from the first—a good excuse to run. Yes, I met Mrs. Rohmer that day. She'd been Mrs. Rohmer for about eight years, during about five of which she used that name as a courtesy title only. You saw her on the eve of becoming Mrs. Mason Gates. Gates was so good a match that at long last she was willing to loosen the financial clutches she still had on me. She had ordered me to Washington at *her* convenience to discuss the matter.

"Now I believe she is Mrs. Rohmer-Gates-Hardwick or something of the sort." Under the edge of the bandages, his mouth looked thin and cruel.

"The mistakes a man commits in his impressionable youth, Erica, can be painful—painful sometimes to the point that thereafter he avoids other emotional ties. But you were so different—" His voice changed then as he delivered a lightning attack.

"Why, Erica, are you so afraid of becoming a woman?"

He gave me no time to man my defenses. The truth burst painfully out of me—

"I am afraid of—of letting go."

"Yes, you have always been afraid of that. So was I back then—a little—maybe that's what attracted me to you—no demands upon me while I was still licking my wounds and pulling my failure around me the way my ancestors clung to their blankets. When I saw Georgia in Washington—well, it made me suspicious of any tie again. *She* did have some reservations about my race. I saw you, yes, and at that moment I didn't want anything to do with any woman—she had thrown some of what she had thought to be home truths at me. So— later when I discovered you gone, and no message—I didn't try any further. Just after that I was posted overseas—the first time I was nosing along Newson's trail, really. So we ran—in opposite directions. But we can't run this time, Erica—we've both got to face fears and facts."

"All right." I fought to keep my outward control. "I'll admit that I ran—want to run now—is that what you want me to confess? I don't want to be involved again." But was that the truth? He was rushing me along. I could not be sure of anything—certainly not of myself.

"Don't you?"

I could no longer meet his eyes as I confessed what I never thought I would ever say aloud:

"I let myself—care for you. I never even told Aunt Otilda about you. When I saw you with—your wife—I knew I could not compete. She was everything I was not. I never could understand why you singled me out—I was nothing to interest a man like you."

"You little fool!" Mark's voice was near savage. "You saw nothing about yourself except what self-pity and cowardice let you see."

"Maybe," I replied. His contempt, or so I read it, was bracing to me. "To have someone—to believe that someone is interested in you when he is not—it gives one a black morning after."

Somehow I felt released, calm. As if I could stand up, walk away, forget I had made a fool of myself for the second time.

"Feel better?" he asked. "Haven't you heard *anything* I've been saying, Erica? You've been so busy scuttling away from shadowy lurkers in your life, you are blind. We're alike, I think, too apt to be self-critical when it comes to emotions. Now that's decided, let's have dinner—"

"What's decided?"

Again a sharp look, which I began to realize, held both impatience and embarrassment.

He reached in his pocket and brought out a small box. Snapping it open he took out a plain band ring, studied it critically for a moment. Then, before I could evade his reach, he caught my hand, spread it out palm up and dropped the ring into the hollow.

"I've been carrying that—perhaps as what you pale-faces call a talisman. Look at it, *pakahi!*"

I obeyed his order. A band of gold, and around it a series of letters very deeply etched, meant to last a long time—a lifetime.

"O-t-s-e-e-t-s-o-h-k-é-m-a-n," I spelled. "What does it mean?"

Mark smiled slowly, with such warmth I had not seen for a long time.

"Something of my people, *pakahi*. In the good old days when we were the only so-called Americans, war-riors of standing took more than one wife. But there was always the *'otseet-sohkéman.'*" He gave the strange words a rich rolling sound as if he relished speaking them. "Direct translation is 'sits-beside-him-wife,' she who did that on all formal occasions. I am enough of a traditionalist to have a fancy for an *ot-seet-sohkéman* of my own, *pakahi*, even if she reigns alone in my lodge."

"And what is a *'pahaki'?*" I stumbled over the word, wary of his challenge.

" 'Little woman'—prosaically enough. Of course, we use it with a warmer meaning than it sounds." His smile grew broader. "I'm flying to England on business the first of February. But there is no reason why my wife cannot accompany me. Will your research be done by then?"

At last I understood. There would never be very many words between us. Words for us both were defenses to hide behind. I did not have an articulate lover—but what I wanted—yes, what I wanted!

I tried to match his tone, though I fear I wavered a little.

"I see no reason why it should not."

Mark arose abruptly and came around the table. It was good there were no other early diners—though I do not believe he would have noticed had a banquet been in progress—nor would have I.

One certainly did *not* need words, I speedily discovered—as the lurker in my shadows came at last into the open, and, I discovered, need not be feared at all.

FREE
Fawcett Books Listing

There is Romance, Mystery, Suspense, and Adventure waiting for you inside the Fawcett Books Order Form. And it's yours to browse through and use to get all the books you've been wanting . . . but possibly couldn't find in your bookstore.

This easy-to-use order form is divided into categories and contains over 1500 titles by your favorite authors.

So don't delay—take advantage of this special opportunity to increase your reading pleasure.

Just send us your name and address and 35¢ (to help defray postage and handling costs).